A Tale of Wind and Sand

K.T. Munson

ISBN 9798576278572

1st Edition

Cover art by Maheen Sana
Copyedited by Tanya Egan Gibson

Dedication

For Grandma Karen.

Other Books by K.T. Munson

1001 Islands
Frost Burn (Coauthored)
North & South
Unfathomable Chance

The Gate Trilogy

The Gate Guardian's Daughter (prequel)
The Sixth Gate
The Nowhere Gate
The King's Gate

Zendar Collection

Zendar: A Tale of Sand (prequel)
Zendar: A Tale of Blood and Sand

Chapter 1:
"Booze and Revenge"

The tavern was alive with the noises of drunken merriment. This oasis amongst the endless sands was known for its pirates and its cheap liquor. It bore no name, for it needed none. It was also the last stop along the edge of the Wasteland. Most did not venture there because the creatures that roamed in those sands were hungry and volatile.

Titus took a sip of his watered-down drink and frowned at the amber liquid. He'd fallen far and he knew it. Hiding from his shame, he was letting boredom and booze rot him away. When the monotony became unbearable, he fought or hunted in the Wasteland. Being the son of a Liege, he'd had the best training in weaponry that any man could have hoped for, an education he now used to win coin at brawls so he could afford to drown his misery as he contemplated revenge.

His half-sister Azel's face flashed in his mind's eye, and he gripped the glass tighter. She and her wretched offspring had ruined him.

"You break it, you buy it," said the bartender, Orik. He was a tall man with rippling biceps and not a hair on him.

Titus relaxed his hand. The man was a son of Imoten, his skin as invincible as steel. It would not be wise to test him.

Hearing the tavern door clatter open and some of the chatter die, Titus turned from where he sat at the bar. The man standing on the threshold wore fine clothes embroidered with gold—a dangerous gamble in such a place as this—and an impatient expression. Titus wondered how long it would take for him to be robbed.

No one barred his passage as he went straight to Orik. "I'm looking for a man," he said, standing a few stools down from Titus. He leaned on the bar. "A man who knows his way into the Wasteland."

"Why would you want to go there?" Orik asked roughly, crossing his arms.

"That's my business," the man replied, but his voice was jovial. "I have a bag of coins for the man who gets me to where I want to go and back again."

"What are you looking for there?" a tall, very dark-skinned man asked.

The man turned with his hands on his hips. "A massive rock supported by a narrow plateau."

Luck usually passed Titus right by, yet he happened to know exactly the place the man meant. He'd seen it once on a salvage run. "How big of a bag?" he asked, ignoring jeers from the other patrons.

The man reached into his cloak and produced a goblet-sized leather drawstring bag. "This big."

Immediately half the tavern was on their feet. The room grew deathly quiet. "I'm thinking you're going to want to hand that bag over," Orik told the wealthy stranger. "If anyone breaks anything they pay for it or answer to me."

"I don't think that will be necessary," the man said calmly. Titus immediate lost interest, knowing exactly how this would end, he turned back to his drink.

Titus heard the door open once more. As he turned, a tall, thin woman walked in. Her ebony hair was short in the back and long in the front. It once would have been odd to see a grown woman with so little hair as was expected in the major cities and inner palaces of which he was accustomed, but now it was normal. From the look of the blade on her hip, she was a woman of the wastes.

"I think all of you should sit down." Her voice was surprisingly hard.

A sudden, heavy breeze passed through the room as she betrayed herself as a daughter of the Lin Bloodline. Those of the Lin Bloodline could manipulate the air around them. Some fell to their knees and others back into their chairs. Though they cursed and protested, few of them had any real power—nothing close to packing such a punch as what Titus could feel in the air from her. Instead of exciting him, the thought of abilities and the Bloodlines left bitterness in his mouth, the aftertaste a reminder of what he'd once had.

The man sat down next to Titus. "You seem like a good fellow." The man set the gold purse next to him on the counter. "I'll offer this to you first."

"Why would I risk my neck for you?" Titus asked, finishing the last of his drink and setting the glass sharply on the counter.

The man leaned closer, as though sharing a secret. "It isn't just about gold but about power. I've spent the better part of my life searching for the path the Bloodline founders took. Have you ever craved power?"

A flash of longing snaked through him. Titus wanted his ability back more than anything—the promise of forever his Corvinus Bloodline had once afforded him. It was his key to revenge and retrieving what had been wrongfully taken from him.

"People around here call me Ti," Titus said, offering the man a hand, "but to my friends I am Titus."

The man smiled as they shook in greeting. "Yevik." He nodded his head toward the dark-haired woman in the door, who was keeping the bar in check with a barrier of harder air. Their fellow patrons protested at being held in place, but quietly, to have power was to be feared. "She is Ven."

"Where is this place you seek?" They stood, and Yevik strode toward the door with Titus by his side.

"I go to the Heart of Zendar," Yevik replied.

Titus shook his head. "A story, nothing more, but I will take you to your balancing rock."

Ven joined them as Yevik pointed to a great flying ship like those Titus' father had commissioned. It was the first time he'd thought of his father in months. Though some part of Titus regretted having to kill the old man, another part knew the Liege Leoric had seen Titus as his greatest shame. Just as Vashdi had. With both gone now, only Azel remained a thorn in his side, his other half siblings were hardly worth a spare thought. Hatred wound itself around his gut at the thought of her and Aryia, her she-devil offspring. The pair of them deserved to suffer as he had.

"Stories have to come from somewhere," Yevik said as they walked aboard the flying ship. "And from someone." The ship crawled with servants and thugs as Yevik led them toward the back of it. "Long before the Bloodlines, Zendar beat to its own rhythm, caring for man but not fully embracing us. As for man, he abused our planet's goodness and natural bounty. In the end, it was man that paid." He opened a door with a flourish, and they stepped into an ornate but functional office. "There was a time before sand and sun, a time when

Zendar had another name and it was science that kept this dying planet alive. And I believe it was science that made the Heart of Zendar."

Titus glanced at Ven, suddenly worried about what he'd agreed to. "Who are you people?"

"Zendar has many secrets," Yevik replied as he picked up a book and held it out. "All of them recorded by scribes."

Titus stepped forward to take the tome in his dirty hands. The spine was soft from use, and when Yevik released it the book opened. It was covered in barely legible scribbles, but most of it Titus recognized as ancient text from his studies as a boy. Frowning, Titus flipped through a few pages. A drawing caught his eye—strange trees that Titus had never seen accompanied by descriptions of how they were made from nature and metal. Odd blue lights twisted and shimmered around them. He felt in his bones, and with sudden unfounded certainty, that he would see this place. It would somehow change him, and he would give birth to a new Bloodline.

Titus snapped the book closed. "I'm in."

Chapter 2:
"Broken Heart"

Bella clasped hands with her sister-by-marriage, Azel, as tears silently streamed down her face. Bandon had been far too young to die. Yet he had, and now she was left all alone. She couldn't look at his face anymore—a face so sweet it might have just been sleeping. Sobbing and covering her face with her hand, she turned into Azel's embrace, forced to the side by Azel's very pregnant stomach. Instantly, the feeling of maternal comfort enveloped her.

Azel let go of Aryia's hand and rubbed Bella's back as final rites were performed for Bandon. Her husband had always been sickly, but in the last few weeks he had been stronger. She'd thought it had meant he was getting better. She'd believed it right up until she'd awoken in the morning to find him stone cold in his chair on the balcony.

"I'm here for you," Azel whispered. "We are all here for you."

Such boundless love made her chest ache as it mingled with her grief. "Why did he have to go?" Bella moved back far enough to see Azel's face.

Azel sighed. "Zendar takes and it gives." Concern filled her beautiful face. "Try to cherish the memories you have with Bandon."

"Has his father been told?" Bella asked. The only person who may be as heartbroken as she was might be Bandon's father, Kavil, the Liege of Momby.

A myriad of expressions danced across Azel's striking features. "He'll be here for the burial tomorrow evening."

Bella cried through the rest of the ceremony. Tomorrow his father would take his remains back to Bandon's former home, Momby. There, they would bury her husband out in the sand so that his soul could return to Zendar, their beloved planet. She was thankful that she didn't have to say her final goodbyes today; she couldn't handle it.

When the memorial was finished, she insisted on staying. For a moment, she took in the fine plants and the soft flowers that surrounded her. She loved the gardens and she liked to think Bandon had loved spending time with her in them. Some of her happiest memories were within the flowering courtyard.

She walked up to the table. She could make out his features despite the shroud. "I loved you," Bella said softly, her fingers brushing against the fabric where his hand was. "When you first arrived I was so disappointed, but you made me hope. I wish I hadn't wasted so much time in the beginning. You made me so happy, and I hope you didn't regret marrying me. Because I don't regret…marrying you..." The last few words were strangled by a sob.

Dissolving into another fit of tears, she knelt beside his cloaked body. He had accepted her completely, loved her without condition, and she had grown to love him over the two years they had been bound in marriage. At the beginning she had thought he, the youngest prince of Momby, didn't deserve her, the princess and sister to the Liege of the three most powerful cities: Sol, Nova, and Undel. Bandon had been the sickly prince with no abilities, and although Bella had not had any of her own at sixteen, back then she'd thought she'd still had time. By now, though, at eighteen, it was unlikely.

Bandon had helped her in so many ways. Now, kneeling beside his lifeless body, she knew she was the undeserving one.

Behind her she heard voices and the shuffling of feet. Unwilling to have her grieving interrupted, she desperately wiped her cheeks and bolted for the safety of a copse of trees. Her fingers grazed rough bark as she knelt in the mossy grass next to one of the trees. Rocking in silence, she swallowed her sobs. The sun shifted in the sky, telling her she had been crying for some time. As her mind wandered, memories melded with dreams.

<>

Bella laughed from where she sat on Bandon's lap as he tried to slow the wild roll of the wheels on his chair. From behind them, Azel called out, but Bella could barely hear it over their laughter. They were invincible. When they hit the sand, the chair turned over and they rolled out of it. The merriment didn't even cease when Bandon landed half across her legs.

"You are crazy," Bandon said, but his eyes shone with love.

Round and round the memories went. Their first kiss. The first time they had lain together as husband and wife. The way he touched her scar and told her she was a gift and that children didn't matter. She could still see the way his dark brown hair would flop in his face as he lay across her stomach. In many ways, he was her closest friend. More memories and more laughter. Two years filled to the brim with it.

When she opened her eyes, she was nestled between two tree trunks. Blinking, she tried to remember why she was there in the dark. Had she fallen asleep playing Little Shadow with Aryia again? Then it hit her square in the chest, Bandon was dead. Again tears sprung to her eyes as she hugged her legs to her chest, burying her face in her knees.

When would this pain end?

"Bella?" a rough voice called. "Azobella?"

It was rare that anyone called her by her full name. "Here," she said weakly. Clearing her throat, she sat up. "I'm here."

Draken rounded the corner, his normally stony expression riddled with concern. "How long have you been here? Everyone has been looking for you."

"Sorry, Drake," she said with a sigh. "I dozed off."

By way of answer he reached out a hand for her, not commenting on the nickname she hadn't used in years. He'd always made her feel so small and young. Her brother, Aleron, did that, too, but with Draken it was different. Her brother could be playful and loving with her, but Draken was all hard edges. Still, though he was gruff and unwieldy with everyone, she trusted him like another older brother.

When she attempted to stand, her legs felt stiff from being folded beneath her for so long. Her left foot tingled as blood rushed back into it. With a curse she hobbled on one leg while she tightened her grip on Draken's arm. He curled it half around her to support her while lifting the lantern.

"Does your brother know you can curse like that?" Draken asked. To her surprise, there was a level of amusement in his eyes.

With a half grin she straightened. "He taught me half of them."

When she turned her head toward the light his lips tugged downward. Before she could react, his knuckle brushed the tears away from her right cheek. Bella blinked in surprise at how tender he was being, let alone that he was being that way with *her*.

“Time will heal your wounds,” Draken said softly, his words almost inaudible. And just like that she knew it would—maybe not today, or tomorrow, but one day.

Relief and hope flooded through her as she put a hand on his chest. “Thank you.”

He nodded, his expression solemn. Unexpectedly, a yawn escaped her. As though remembering himself, he shifted back from her and his usual mask of indifference returned. Had she imagined the previous warmth? Was she still dreaming?

When he continued to keep his arm so it could support her, she knew it hadn’t been her imagination. She limped a little, and he helped her from the shadowy groove. Moments before she’d been terrified, but something about his confidence and size now made her feel safe. No it wasn’t just that, it was because she knew he would protect her—had protected her.

When someone called her name, Draken called out, “I have her.”

Suddenly, two maids appeared, and the intimacy of the moment was broken. They immediately voiced how worried they were. When they moved closer to inspect her and tried to usher her away, she tightened her hold on Draken, terrified to return to her room—their room.

“I…” Bella began, gazing up at Draken’s hard face.

“You scared me half to death!” Azel called out to her, appearing behind the maids. Beautiful, wonderful Azel was angry, but Bella couldn’t be more relieved to see her sister-by-marriage. Before Bella could respond, she was wrapped in a crushing hug, Azel’s round belly between them. “You are staying with me tonight,” Azel declared. “I already had a bath drawn. Let’s get you cleaned up.” She extracted a crunched dried leaf from Bella’s hair.

Where the two handmaids had done nothing to assuage her fear, Azel filled her to the brim with happiness and security. Sometimes Bella wondered what their lives would be like if Azel hadn’t come into it nearly four years earlier. She honestly didn’t like to even imagine that kind of reality. Zendar was at peace, and Bella had a family who loved her. Not to mention that Azel was of the Vandi Bloodline and had one of the most terrifying abilities in all of Zendar. If something did happen, she could defend them from nearly any attack. Bella only wished Azel could cure a broken heart.

Chapter 3:
“Reckless”

Thirteen months later

Bella shrieked as her twin cousins giggled and chased her in the small palace courtyard. Oren and Ewan were barely a year old, but they were fast. Bella knew they were going to be like Aleron, as powerful as a true member of house Kaheron. Aryia sat with a book in her lap on a bench they’d moved next to a pillar to shade them from the sun, her illegitimate half-brother Verik beside her. They had already played Little Shadow with the twins, and it was her turn to distract them while Azel and Aleron saw to stately business. Verik’s older brother, Le’Roy, was behind them, giving chase.

Draken’s sister, Lycin, had brought them from Nova for the Festival of the Sun, which ushered in the dry season when they would gather and store as much water as possible and stockpile the plants gathered at the earlier harvest. It also started the second growing season within the massive glass growing houses, when most of the fruit was sweetest. It was by far Bella’s favorite time of year.

The twins yelled, “Catch!” One of the few words they knew.

Le’Roy mock yelled before sprinting the last distance to her. He caught her around the waist and spun her around. Though he was nearly five years younger than her, he was tall and strong like Aleron. She could see her brother in his face.

“Put me down.” Bella fought him, but it was halfhearted.

Bella was still laughing when the ground began to shake. Screams filled the air. “Aryia, Verik, Oren, Ewan. Come here!” Bella shouted.

“What is it?” Le’Roy shouted.

The trees shook as Le’Roy stumbled backwards, and Bella fell to her knees, protectively wrapping her arms around the twins, who had thankfully been close to her. There was shouting, and someone screamed. Bella could see Aryia next to Verik, trying to help him stand as dust rained down from the ceiling and pillar. Bella’s chest felt tight and her stomach was in knots as she felt a blind need to go to her niece.

"Aryia!" Bella yelled, her heart in her throat. Aryia didn't cry out, but her eyes were wide with fear. Bella thrust the twins into Le'Roy's arms. "Protect them."

"What?" Le'Roy asked as the boys clung to him and wailed.

Bella stumbled toward Aryia and Verik, her legs unsteady. The ground jerked under her feet, and her knees hit the ground. She caught herself with her hands. A flash of green and purple was followed by an explosion of pain on her back. Trapped under one of the many flowering trees in the garden, Bella tried to focus, but she was having trouble breathing. Painstakingly, she crawled out from under the fallen tree, the destroyed purple flowers scattered on the ground around her. The rumbling slowed as she reached Aryia and Verik, whose backs were pressed against the pillar. She wrapped her arms around them, shielding both of the children with her body.

"Bella?" Aryia asked, her tone filled with dread.

Her words seemed so far away. Bella slumped over them as the edge of her vision darkened. She heard yelling and perhaps words she should recognize, but they were lost in the sea of hurt. Suddenly, she felt a strong arm around her waist. Someone picked up her limp body. The person was saying something but she couldn't understand, the pain so intense that it drowned everything out. Someone else was yelling. It was a deep voice. Aleron?

She saw Azel's face, and warmth filled her. Suddenly, she could breathe again. "It was a rib," she heard Azel say, her comforting hands on Bella's side. "You were right to bring her to me. Where are the children?"

Bella held on to her brother. "I tried…" she began before she lost consciousness.

<>

"Greetings, Bella," Bandon said, a sweet smile on his face.

"Bandon?" Bella could barely breathe. Months had passed since she'd dreamt of him. For a moment she didn't know what seemed so strange, but then she realized he didn't look sick. He was standing tall and proud without any sign of fatigue.

"I have missed you, my love," Bandon said softly, his voice so tender.

Tears sprung to Bella's eyes as she choked out, "Why did you have to go?"

"It was time. I only held on as long as I did because of you," Bandon told her, light seeming to emanate from him. "But it is time for you to live."

With a halting sob, Bella reached for him, her fingers desperate to touch him and feel that familiar warmth. Gasping, she opened her eyes. Tears streamed down the side of her face and pooled on the pillow by her ears. When she went to raise her hands to her face to wipe away the tears, she realized something was holding her left arm down.

To her left, a dark shape slept on the chair, his arm extended and his big hand resting across her arm. Memories of what had happened earlier came rushing back as she remembered why her brother would be there. Wiping her tears away, Bella reached across with her other hand to shake him awake. Wait, she realized, pulling her hand away. It wasn't Aleron. Draken's face was set in sleep as though something was troubling him.

Could it have been Draken that saved her? Bella wondered.

She rolled onto her side and sucked in a hiss of air at the pain the movement brought forth. She grasped her side as Draken roused from his sleep. When Draken focused on her face he looked concerned—she could see it finely etched on his face.

"Should I get Azel?" Draken asked.

"No," Bella rolled back onto the bed. Though her side was tender, she could breathe normally. "Was it you who helped me?"

He hesitated. "Yes."

Bella huffed out a laugh. "I thank you. You haven't had to protect me like that in a long time. Is everyone well?"

He nodded and half grunted in response. "They're fine. Very few injuries. One of the guards was killed."

Bella tried to readjust how she was sitting on the bed. "I didn't even know you were there."

"Aryia called for me," Draken replied by way of explanation. "After the shaking stopped."

Wrestling with the blankets, Bella tried to move as little as possible while still getting into a more comfortable position. Draken must have realized she was struggling because he wordlessly reached over and fixed her pillows. She caught his scent, heady and virile, the complete opposite of Bandon. Draken smelled like earth. Time slowed as Bella suddenly became aware of how close he was. She stared at his jaw—had it always been so attractive?

"I thank you," Bella whispered.

Draken grunted before straightening, and just like that the spell was broken. Blinking, Bella realized she must have hit her head as well. Draken was not someone she would consider handsome. He was too big and gruff. Not at all like Bandon.

"I appreciate you staying with me," Bella said softly. "But you don't need to stay anymore. I know there are others to see to."

He nodded once and left. The room that had once seemed so comfortable suddenly felt empty. Shrinking back further into pillows, Bella tugged the thin blanket up to her throat and tried to get some rest.

Chapter 4:
"Festival of the Sun"

Bella frowned as she lifted her leg out of the bath. A bruise she hadn't noticed before was purpling on her calf. Beside her, Azel was talking with Aryia as she brushed her hair. After another day of rest, Bella was happy to be up and about again, especially considering it was the day of the Festival of the Sun. It was one of Bella's favorites, and levity was much needed after the recent quake. After that they would fly to Nova and spend the summer in the slightly colder secondary capital. In the corner the twins were splashing each other as they played with glass beads the size of their fists, too big to put in their mouths.

"Will there be dancing like last year?" Aryia asked, drawing Bella's attention.

Azel nodded. "And masks."

"Do I still get a sun mask?" Aryia asked with the most excitement Bella had heard in her voice in a while.

"Same one as last year. You won't get your new one for a few years," Azel replied.

"Mine!" Oren shrieked as he took it away from his brother.

With a sigh, Azel grabbed a towel and strode across the bath. Despite having given birth to three children, Azel, with her honeyed skin and sleek black hair, was the most beautiful woman Bella had ever seen. She could still remember the first bath they had shared all those years ago. It was as though she'd barely aged a day. There were subtle changes, like the lines on her stomach, but they were hardly noticeable.

"Time to get out." Azel picked Oren up and began drying off his head. "Hadi," she called, "the boys are done."

Bella admired that about Azel. Most women of wealth and power didn't have time to care for their children, but Azel made a point to tend to them. From bathing to meals, Azel was almost always there, and Aleron usually made it to dinner, where they ate as a family. There were a few exceptions but the routine was nice. It made her feel like she was part of the family instead of feeling alone.

When Aleron's bastards, Le'Roy and Verik were in town, Azel even let them join in. Unlike usual queens, Azel hadn't had them assassinated or exiled once she'd married Aleron. Instead, she'd invited them into her home. Lycin, their mother and Draken's sister was no longer afforded such luxury, but that was only because she'd been blatantly disrespectful towards Azel. So her children were allowed within the walls, but she was not except on festival days. Good riddance—Bella had never cared for her haughty attitude and the less she saw of her the better.

By the time she brought her attention back to the room, the twins were gone and Azel was helping Aryia dry off. When her daughter left, Azel sunk back into the bath and watched her go. With a sigh, she turned and propped her elbows on the edge of the bath as she let her head fall back.

"They can be such a handful, but my goodness do I love them." Azel smirked at Bella at the last part.

Bella leaned forward. "Think you'll have more soon?"

Azel released an incredulous laugh. "If Aleron has his way, he'd have a small army. The twins were a hard birth, though, so I'd like a little time to pass before the next one." Bella laughed with her. "What about you? How have you been?"

Bella blinked in surprise. "I'm doing well."

"Still having nightmares?" Azel asked. Bella felt her inspecting her face.

Bella shrugged. "Rarely."

"We haven't talked about it in a while." Azel moved closer as her voice dropped.

"You were right." Bella stared across the opulent bath past the potted plants and pale pink curtains. "I will marry again."

Azel touched a hand to her arm. "Have anyone in mind?"

Bella's mind flashed to Draken's face as he'd bent close to her. Averting her eyes, Bella answered, "No."

<>

Bella stared at the two dresses on her bed. She had worn so much white in the last few months that she was tired of it. It had been more than six months, so a respectful time had passed, but she'd continued to wear the color of mourning. Her eyes shifted to the black dress with silver and red adornments. It was her favorite because it made her petite breasts seem bigger than they were. After her dream a few days earlier involving Bandon, she'd considered wearing the second dress, knowing it would invite compliments.

Was she ready? The question had kept her up two nights in a row.

With a heavy sigh, she picked up the white dress and slowly started to put it on. She was not a brave woman, not like her dear sister-by-marriage Azel. Without a doubt, Bella knew Azel would have chosen the black one. Halfway dressed Bella paused. She might not be as brave as Azel, but she could at least admit her mourning period had passed.

Bella wriggled out of the dress and tossed it on the bed by the provocative one. Returning to her closet, she scanned the dresses until she found a deep purple and gold one. She plucked it from the closet and admired the little suns woven into the neckline. She unclipped the belt and pulled it over her head, adjusting the ornate collar so the scooped back was set, and then threaded her arms through the sheer sleeves that had a long slits from her shoulder to her wrist, where they ended in a beaded cuff. Once she'd secured them on each wrist, Bella fastened the strap, accenting her trim waist. She twirled once, causing the bottom edges of the elegant skirts to float, for moment, above the ground.

With a contented sigh, she straightened the fabric, feeling comfortable. These clothes were what Bella was used to—not ones for inviting men but no longer ones for mourning her dead husband. It was a compromise she was happy with. She put in gold earrings that matched the gold adornments on her outfit. Taking a veil in the event the sun was still up, Bella took one final look at her tan skin and dark brown hair that framed her young face in the handheld mirror. It was tarnished on one spot, marring her cheek, but given that there weren't many personal mirrors left, she was thankful to have it.

She set the mirror down, grabbed her mask, and hurried down the hall toward the royal apartments. She stopped in the hallway when she saw Aleron in a doorway. He was talking with someone, and just from the expression on his face, Bella knew who it was. Azel went on her tiptoes to kiss him. That was the kind of love Bella wanted again.

Azel watched him walk away, a smitten smile across her lips. When she shifted to return to her room, Bella spoke up. "Good evening."

"Bella," Azel said warmly. She could see Azel immediately take her all in, including her outfit. Azel's lips to spread into a wide grin. "I've never been so happy to see purple."

Bella quickly fell into her warm embrace. "It was time." She suddenly felt shy at her boldness—someone may ask her dance. "Where is Aleron going?"

"To do what he always does," Azel answered cryptically before turning back into the room with a laugh.

Bella loved the Festival of the Sun and the way it heralded in their summer months. It was the end of their primary growing season before the temperatures were too hot. The massive glass houses slowly harvested their plants until only those accustomed to the excessive temperatures remained—primarily fruit. All sorts of food were stored within the innards of the massive rocky plateaus.

Azel was already wearing a gold and black outfit that matched her massive golden earrings and headdress. On most women it would seem flashy and gaudy, but on Azel it was perfect, complimenting her stunning beauty. In contrast, Bella wore few adornments. Within the room Aryia was seated on the bed, a book open as she read by candlelight, her sun mask on the bed beside her.

"We had better go," Azel said, knocking on the door.

A stream of handmaids streamed in, chattering away with excitement. Already their masks were in place, and they moved to help Bella, Azel, and Aryia secure their own. Azel's was not a mask but more of a massive decorative crown that rested on her head and framed her face. Bella's was a half mask, covering only the right side of her face with a decorative sun.

Once they were ready, Azel led them from the room and to the doors that led out into the street. The sun was beginning to set, casting the courtyard in gold. It shined off Azel's metal headdress as Aleron turned back to her. He was dressed in gold and white, his own crown spiked and tipped in pearls. Beside him, Draken wore a half-gray mask, representing the moon, his stern face and bulky form impossible to miss.

When Aleron held a hand out to Azel, the crowd began to cheer, calling both to the Liege Aleron and his beautiful bride. They were beloved of the people, having brought peace to Zendar. More than once Bella had seen people approach Azel in the street to receive blessings from her. It was a wonderful time to be alive.

After Azel and Aleron boarded the massive open carriage, their children joined them, and then Bella and the members of the royal guard, including Draken. The people threw petals and cheered as they rode down the main street. Behind them, some of the recent harvest was passed out to those in the street. Aleron and Azel waved as the twins watched, wide-eyed, at all the people.

It was a relatively new tradition, this being only their fifth year doing such an event, but it was quickly becoming Bella's favorite. The risk of such a procession had been too great before due to fear of assassins; it would have made Aleron too easy of a target. Azel, however, had changed all of that. Though Bella still felt a slight lingering fear, her hand instinctively touching the place where she'd been stabbed, with each year that passed without incident her trepidation lessened.

The streets were filled with merriment as they made their rounds, bread was passed out, and three big vats of wine were ladled into waving cups and bowls. Bella tried to be happy, but this was the first year she'd participated alone. Suddenly the crowds she normally was excited to see, felt daunting. There was a happy medium—where safety existed. When they returned home, she let out a sigh of relief. Her entire body sagged as she felt the stress flow out of her.

She scrambled over the side and returned to the safety of their palace, the twins rushing past her, shouting, with Aryia and Verik following close behind. Bella paused at the door as the progression moved through the main hall and into the grand entertainment hall. In the past, before Azel became queen, it had been full of dancing scantily clad women and late-night brawls. Though there was still the occasional brawl, the women that danced now were at least fully dressed. Much to Bella's relief.

Aryia and Verik giggled in front of her, and she mused how close the pair were, thick as thieves. A dull ache filled her chest as she watched them and was reminded of Bandon. He had been more than her husband—he'd been her closest friend. She missed the companionship he'd given her and their unconditional friendship. Watching Aryia and Verik, it made her realize she didn't have any close friends who weren't family. What did that say about her?

With a sigh, she resolved to enjoy the night or at least try to. It was her favorite festival after all.

Chapter 5:
"Lav-tu"

The drums were pounding in a pulsating rhythm, and Bella couldn't help but sway back and forth in her seat as the dancers told the story of Zendar with only their bodies. The music accented the movements and punctuated an already gripping performance. The women were dressed in tan-colored clothing to match the sands of Zendar; as they danced around, men fell to the sands and were lost until only seven remained.

She could remember watching this dance as a child, the portrayal of the Julius and Vandi Bloodlines. Each side wore terrifying masks and were portrayed as evil. Azel had put a stop to that. History was history, she had told them, and be it Julius or Kaheron or Vandi, they all had their part to play. Now, the story they told was whole and unbiased. Bella preferred it that way as well, even if she was without a Bloodline of her own.

The dance came to a climax with a final drumming sequence that seemed to beat in time with her heart and then drove faster and louder until a resounding *bam* echoed off the walls. The audience began to clap and cheer. Raised thumbs could be seen all around the room.

"People of Sol," the announcer called out, "give thanks to our Liege and his bride." The applause for the dancers paled in comparison to the homage their people gave to their leader. It warmed Bella's heart to know that people's fear of Aleron and Azel was clearly secondary to their love for them. "On this auspicious day we gather to wish our beloved leaders goodbye for the next six months while they toil away in Nova." There were boos and sighs of sadness. "The sun sets on Sol, but our Liege leaves us in the hands of his most trusted advisor, Hadish."

Bella's craned her neck to see the handsome man. He was ten years Aleron's senior but charmingly handsome. He was clever by all accounts, and Bella recalled her foolish childhood crush with burning cheeks. She could remember wishing very much that Hadish Solomon would take her as a bride. There was something she'd always fancied about older men.

It was rare she saw him and Aleron in the same place at the same time, as when one was in Sol the other was in Nova or vice versa. It was only at events like today's festival that Bella caught glimpses of him.

Bella had been so distracted that she'd missed the rest of the announcer's speech. When Aleron stood, silence immediately fell throughout the room, drawing her attention. Even though he was her brother, she, too, was in awe of his powerful presence.

"We gather on this day of celebration to honor Zendar," Aleron's voice boomed above the hushed din. "To honor the harvest and the sun. To be thankful for what we have and celebrate those who are dear to us." Aleron lifted a glass. "I lift a glass to our continued peace and prosperity."

"Peace and prosperity!" The crowd cheered, drinking from their cups.

The music immediately started and Aleron and Azel moved to the dance floor. This had become Bella's favorite part—their dance. Aleron had never taken much part in the dancing before Azel, as without a wife the Lav-tu could not be done. Despite the ritual of the dance and the simplicity of the music, the two of them somehow brought another dimension to it.

Aleron's palms met Azel's as they pushed back and forth against each other, faster and faster in time with the beat of the drum. The chiming of Azel's mask was unmistakable at first and then was drowned out by the rhythmic thudding. They froze before a call was heard and Azel bent forward to allow Aleron's robes to cover her.

"The world was dark, and man was sad," a voice called. "Until the great Sol rose in the sky and proclaimed that light should fill the valleys and kiss the mountains of Zendar." Azel appeared from his arms, and slowly Aleron took her by the waist and raised her up. She held her arms in a circle above her head to let her clothing block her mask from view. "Sol loved Zendar so completely that when he kissed her the oceans of water became oceans of sand. The waves were replaced with dunes, and man suffered once more, but never from the lack of light and warmth. Saddened by what the mighty sun had done, Zendar looked upon her children and beckoned them into her bosom."

Aleron lowered Azel until their lips touched, and it was like a lightning strike through the crowd. Dancers with long sheer beige ribbons danced around Azel and Aleron, and dramatic drumming filled the air. Azel danced away from him, her dress and jewelry chiming as children appeared on stage. All the Liege's children went to the stage, including Verik, whose hand was linked with Aryia's. Seeing them brought a warmness to her heart.

"Zendar reached out with a powerful hand and gifted each so that they might lead." The storyteller's words faded as she fought back the flood of her emotions. Last year he'd been sitting beside her at this event and holding held her hand. Tears threatened at his memory.

While many stood and cheered, Bella turned away. "Isn't he handsome?" Lycin's voice cut into her thoughts.

Blinking back her tears, Bella straightened in surprise. Lycin was rarely welcome in the palace, and it had been some time since Bella had spoken to her. Even more surprising was she had taken the seat directly next to Bella at the honored table.

"Who?" Bella asked, glancing at the stage and her brother.

"Le'Roy," Lycin replied with a chuckle. "My son takes after his father."

The loving expression on her face made Bella uncomfortable. Although Lycin had once been Aleron's favored concubine, since Azel had come into his life, he'd dismissed all of his concubines—either for her or because of her.

"He is a good boy."

"Yes," Lycin's face lit up and shone with pride, "I was blessed to have such a son." She finally looked at Bella. "How are you faring? I see you no longer wear the color of mourning."

The words felt like claws around her heart. "Fine," she said, the word coming out a croak. She cleared her throat. "I am managing."

Lycin's face softened, and she touched a hand to Bella's shoulder. "I was never able to tell you that I was sorry to hear of his passing. The few times I witnessed you together, it was easy to see it was a happy union."

For a moment Bella was shocked. Lycin had never been so kind to her. "I am grateful for your words," she heard herself say automatically, still stunned by the interaction.

"Mother!" Le'Roy was suddenly next to them. Bella had been so caught up in their discussion that she hadn't noticed the play had ended. "Come and dance with me!"

Lycin smiled, looking the happiest Bella had ever seen her. "Excuse me, Princess."

As Bella watched them dance, a sudden melancholy settled over her. Would she ever be a mother? Her hand touched her side where the mark of an assassin's failed attempt on her life still lay as tears threatened again. Why could she not make herself be happy on this blessed day?

When a wineglass appeared in front of her face, she jerked back in surprise. She glanced up at the hand it was attached to. "This is a time of celebration," Draken informed her. "Drink and be merry. For tomorrow we go to Nova."

She accepted the drink hesitantly, gratitude sweeping through her for the distraction. "Thank you."

Determined to do just that, when the melody turned and others were invited to join on the stage, Bella swallowed the wine in a few quick gulps. She thought to ask Draken to join her, but he had vanished. She stood and finally spotted him across the room talking with his sister, Lycin. Resolved to distract herself, she joined the dancing, something she had not done since Bandon's death. And to her surprise, for the first time in a long time, Bella had fun.

Chapter 6:
"Revenge"

Bella awoke to shouting. For a moment she forgot where she was. She sat up, groggy, and an instant later fear set in. Then it all came flooding back, they were on an airship on their way to Nova. She felt frozen, and her stomach twisted. She tossed the blankets aside, her feet hitting the floor an instant before her door was thrown open.

"Bella!" Azel's dark hair was wild around her face. "We are under attack."

Beside Azel, a wide-eyed but quiet Aryia gripped a blanket around her shoulders with one hand. Her other hand was clasped on her mother's. For the first time, Bella noticed how much Aryia took after Azel.

"Who is attacking us?" Bella asked as Azel turned into the hall.

"We don't know," Azel answered before the ship rocked to the right side. "We have to hurry."

When they exited the room, Hadi and Nitya were waiting with the twin boys. Ewan was crying, while Oren was staring at his mother in abject fear over Nadi's shoulder. His expression was like cold water on her spine, and she momentarily froze. Azel didn't wait for her, barreling ahead.

"We have to get to the flyers," she called out, her voice loud but calm. That was Azel—focused, even when everyone else was panicking.

Bella stood still, her legs locked, her stomach churning. Panicked servants, guests, and guards streamed around her. She felt a scream bubble in her chest.

"Bella!" Azel yelled from the next junction, turning and waving to her.

Just like that, her trance was broken. She ran to them, wishing to hug her sister-by-marriage but determined to retain some dignity. A guard bumped into her, and Bella stumbled back, crashing toward the ground. A gentle feeling overtook her. When she opened her eyes, she was hovering above the ground—held above the floor, a breath from pain.

"Bella, run!" Azel shouted.

The sound of steel behind her drew her attention. She turned to see the guard locked in arms with a man who wore old clothes and carried a sword that was splattered with blood. He went to land a killing blow on the guard and was suddenly thrown backwards. Azel's hair was wild, but her eyes were focused. It was her gift, the Vandi Bloodline, of which everyone was in awe. Scrambling to her feet, Bella dashed the last distance to Azel and safety.

They rounded another corner and were immediately exposed to the view of Zendar. The ship was losing altitude. Wind whipped at the bottom of her clothing, making her bare feet cold. Bella's gaze was drawn to three guards at the end. Nitya was already gone with one of the twins, and Hadi was being loaded into another glider. The wind stung her face as they used the leather grips along the inner hallway to keep their balance.

Suddenly, the airship tipped sharply to the side. Bella screamed, holding on for dear life as her legs dangled. It righted itself a moment later, but it was diving sharply. With surreal clarity, she realized that they were going to crash. Azel pushed off and ran toward the glider containing Hadi and Oren. The two guards that had been standing there were gone, lost among the sands of Zendar.

Hadi was beating her fist against the thick glass door. "Trade places with me, my queen." Despite Azel and Hadi's attempt to open the door it would not give. The mechanism appeared to be broken. Bella's gaze was drawn beyond them as the ground rushed up to meet them.

"There isn't time," Azel replied and pulled the emergency release. The glider shot out away from the ship and into the dunes as Bella wrapped her free hand around Aryia.

Azel looked back at them, her face serene as she stared at Aryia. Her hair danced around her face, and her eyes almost sad. Aryia was yelling something, reaching for her mother as Bella refused to let her go. They were safer the further they could be from the opening, and Azel could protect herself.

"I love…" the words were barely audible a minute before the air ship veered sharply to the side. The rest was screaming, and then sand across her face followed by darkness.

<>

Bella awoke to a suffocating nothingness. She felt weighted down and struggled to free herself from her restraints. Memories overtook disorientation as she freed herself from the sand. Panic settled in as her eyes searched desperately for any sign of light in the all-consuming darkness. Her eyes riveted, finally, to a shaft of light far above her, on the far side, revealing the top of the ladder.

"Azel? Aryia?" Bella called out in hope.

Bella swallowed hard at the desperation and fear in her voice. Panic crawled up her throat, threatening to strangle her. She felt immobilized, trapped, as the darkness seemed to close in around her. Helplessness swamped her, and suddenly she was a child again. Fear choked her as flashes of the assassin from years ago broke down the last of her strength. Bella curled her arms around her legs, making herself into a ball as tears streamed down her face.

Then there was a groan. For a moment Bella thought she'd imagined it. "Hello?" she whispered before licking her dry lips, ears straining.

A hand touched her shoulder. "Do you know where mama is?" Aryia's voice broke the silence. She'd never sounded so young and afraid before.

With sudden clarity, Bella realized she couldn't dwell—she had a young girl to take care of. "I'm here." Bella reached up, feeling for her shoulders in the dark so she could hug her. "Azel was further ahead."

"She might be buried!" Aryia exclaimed, slipping through Bella's grasp. Bella struggled to gain purchase on the girl as she darted away.

"Wait!" Bella felt fear sweep in but Aryia was right—they must search for her.

Standing, Bella hurried after her. Her side hurt, but she seemed to be mostly unharmed. She rushed forward blindly until she tripped. Her heart in her throat, she sprawled on the ground. Reaching back she felt around in the dark, the sand gritty against her hands until she touched something soft.

"Aryia!" Bella yelled as she started digging out what she guessed was Azel's arm. "I found her. Follow my voice."

Bella felt her niece's hands join hers a moment later. Their panting and the movement of the sand punctuated the tense blackness. Focusing on the task instead of her fear, Bella was able to pull Azel's head free shortly after. Bella leaned close to her nose and was relieved to feel shallow breaths come from her. They seemed labored, though, and Azel's skin was peppered with a cold sweat. It was slick under Bella's fingers as she propped Azel's head on her lap. She didn't know how, but Azel was still alive. The question was, though, for how long?

"Please be all right," Aryia whispered over and over as she continued to work to free her mother. Bella could hear her frantic movements.

"She's breathing," Bella choked out. "We need to finish getting her out."

Tears fell freely as they worked to extract her. She lay on her side, her torso buried in the sand, as though it had swept in over her like a wave. Once her upper half was dug out, they were able to pull her free. Bella heaved her free, reaching under her arms and locking across her chest. The three of them huddled there, Azel unconscious, as the other two cried, holding on to the person who was a mother to one of them and a mother figure to the other. Her breathing grew increasingly labored with each inhalation, and their hearts broke over the possible damage.

Suddenly, Aryia's voice broke the pattern. "It is time to wake up." This time her voice was more of a command than a plea.

Bella tightened her hold, trying to think of the right words to say.

"Aryia?" she heard Azel say a moment later. Her voice was quiet, and she sounded confused.

Relief flooded through Bella. Clearly she had missed the mark on how badly Azel had been injured.

"I'm here," Aryia answered as Bella started crying anew, overwhelmed with joy.

"Bella too?" Azel asked, stirring to wrap her arms around them. "Thank Zendar! Are you hurt?" She held them close, whispering words of comfort. After confirming everyone was mostly unscathed, she said, "We need to go."

Bella wiped away her tears, and together they stood. She pointed, even though they couldn't see her. "Up there. That's the way out."

Carefully they made their way in the dark. It was several minutes before they reached the ladder. Azel insisted that Bella start up first. The ship was on its side, so it would not be easy for them to move, but Azel could push them. Reluctantly, Bella agreed.

She was nearly to the top when she heard the distant sounds of chaos. Hands shaking, she situated herself at the top rung. There was an open doorway to her right and the long hallway in darkness to her left. Going as far over as she could, Bella reached for the opening. Her fingers strained to gain purchase on the door's edge.

"You are safe." Azel's voice floated up from below her.

Before Bella could ask what she meant, a gentle feeling overtook her and she was lifted from the ladder and pushed up to the door. Despite the fact that her legs were dangling over the side, Bella wasn't afraid. Azel assured her she was safe, and so she was. No questions asked. She'd protected her once before, brought her back when she'd nearly been poisoned to death.

Once Bella was up in the hallway she realized how horribly they'd crashed. The odd angle of the airship would likely make escaping difficult. Aryia's head appeared, and she soon floated up to join Bella, who helped her up to a corner where the hallway continued. When Azel appeared, Bella realized they had a problem.

"How are you going to get up?" Bella asked looking around.

"We can figure that out shortly. You are going to have to find a rope or something for me to climb," Azel told them, her voice calm and confident. "Let's get you further up."

Aryia floated up to the main hallway, propelled by Azel's gift. Bella didn't know what they would have done if Azel hadn't survived. The thought was chilling as Aryia reached the second hallways.

With a grunt Aryia disappeared for a moment. "I know what to do, Mama," Aryia told her before turning away from them.

"Aryia!" Azel yelled, "Don't go there! Come back." Her formerly calm voice took on a frantic edge. "Bella, you need to go after her."

Bella nodded before situating herself in the hallway to be maneuvered up to where Aryia was. It was like being lifted into someone's arms, as though her body was hers but at the same time, something was propelling her forward. It was a strange sensation, very different from when Azel had healed her. Awkwardly, Bella wiggled herself into the hallway. It was in utter disrepair, but she could see sunlight ahead past a blockage and through another doorway far down the hall. The idea of sunlight felt comforting, but the savage sounds of battle did not.

"Aryia?" Bella asked, taking a step forward.

"Here!" Aryia called from a room to her right.

Slowly making her way along the wall, Bella crouched down and peered into the dark room. A firestone lamp that had been knocked on its side glowed softly. There was a distinct tearing noise. Bella's eyes trained on Aryia. Not for the first time, Bella wished she had a Bloodline of her own to offer assistance.

"What are you doing?" Bella asked, eyeing the tousled room and broken furniture.

"Making rope," Aryia replied.

"How are you going to get back here?" Bella asked, eyeing the floor.

Aryia twisted and knotted the fabric into a long cord. "I won't. You'll tie this off with mama and I'll act like a counterweight."

Disbelief flooded through Bella as she considered their options. What did a six year old know… how could a six year old know all this? Although, admittedly, Aryia had always seemed oddly mature for her age. Bella had always found her a little disconcerting, the way her eyes at times seemed to bore into Bella's very soul.

"I don't know if this is going to work…" Bella began.

Behind her Azel called out, "Is Aryia all right?"

"I'll be right back," Bella told Aryia before making her way back to the other end. Azel was still at the top of the ladder, looking concerned. "Aryia's making a rope from fabric for you. She has a plan." Saying it out loud only made it seem more absurd. In a more hushed tone she added, "I think there is still fighting happening outside. I'm worried about Aleron."

"Aleron can take care of himself," Azel replied, but apprehension passed over her face. "We need to escape before the fighting stops."

"Bella!" Aryia's voice was muffled.

"I'll be back," Bella said to Azel before making her way to the room, feeling like she was being jerked back and forth between mother and daughter.

"Stay back, and I'll throw the end up," Aryia called, causing Bella to pause. A round object attached to a long strip appeared through the doorway before sliding back down. There was a shout and then a crash. Bella rushed to the opening.

"Aryia?"

"I'm fine," Aryia called, sounding annoyed. "I miscalculated. Stay there. I'll try again."

Sitting back on her haunches, she waited. This time when the end appeared, Bella reached out and snagged the cloth. Aryia gave a triumphant cry before telling her to take it to her mother. Without hesitation, Bella returned to where Azel was.

"Here it is," Bella said and let the ball down slowly toward Azel.

When it reached the end, Azel strained to reach it. After two or three tries, she was able to snag the end. She tied it around her waist. Slowly but surely, Azel made her way up. Bella's hands hurt from trying to hold the cloth steady and help haul her up over the side. Relief flooded through her when Azel's head and arms appeared at the edge of the hallway.

"Let me help," Bella said, and it wasn't long before Azel was standing beside her.

"Where is Aryia?" Azel asked as she righted herself and started unfastening their makeshift rope from her waist.

"I'm down here, Mama," Aryia called.

After they worked together to get Aryia out of the room, mother and daughter embraced. Bella wished their trials were over, but something deep within her told her they were just beginning. Despite that looming possibility, though, Bella knew they would be safe with Azel.

Without hesitation, Azel spurned them into action, heading toward the light.

Bella felt utterly disoriented as they picked their way along the corridor. The entire ship was in a state of disarray. Once they reached the end of the hall, they had to stop. The upper deck had caved in, blocking their escape.

"What can you see?" Bella asked as Azel maneuvered herself up to see past the light.

"The ship is broken in half," Azel replied softly as she strained to see more. "I don't see…Oh! There are a row of escape ships."

Azel immediately abandoned the hallway and entered the room to the left. Together they helped each other navigate the odd angle of the room, bracing and heaving to get them all through the door. Unlike the other room, this one had a partial opening. It was narrow, but Bella guessed it was going to be just large enough to crawl through.

"I'll go first," Aryia said, inspecting the opening. When Azel hesitated, Aryia added, "I'm the smallest. Lift me up." There was a determined shine in Aryia's eye, the kind she got when she decided whatever she was saying was going to happen one way or another.

Finally, Azel nodded. Bella let out the breath she hadn't realized she was holding. "Up you go."

Carefully, Aryia went into the opening. After a few minutes they heard Aryia call back softly. "There's a lot of activity on the other side of the ship. And just a small ledge, but we can reach the hoverships."

Azel nodded. "You next."

The hole was full of rubble but it was big enough that Bella easily fit through. For once she was relieved for her slim, almost boyish, figure. Once on the other side she called back to Azel. Azel, while quite fit, was not as small and was curvier, so it took her much longer to get out. Bella hopped from foot to foot nervously as she kept peeking at the pure chaos on the other side of the ship.

When Azel finally joined them, she hurried them toward the escape ships. Bella saw Aryia crane her neck to see what all the noise was about, but Bella just kept her head down. She wanted to get out of there.

When they reached the escape ships, they found that two were damaged below but two others appeared to be in working order. Azel carefully disengaged the door and began ushering them inside one. Aryia immediately sat down and began securing her straps.

Bella paused on the threshold. "You should go with her," Bella protested. "I'll go in the other one."

"There isn't time," Azel replied, pushing her into the craft. "You need to do everything you can to protect her. I—"

"Azel!" someone yelled, cutting her off. "Where are you? Azel!" Azel froze, the blood draining from her face. "I have your Liege."

Azel closed her eyes, taking careful breaths. Bella's stomach was in knots, her hand still pressed against the glass of the glider, keeping the door propped open. When Azel opened her eyes, her earlier indecision was gone.

"When I distract them, you go in the opposite direction," Azel told Bella, gripping her shoulders. "You keep Aryia safe from him. No matter what happens, don't come for me. Promise." She glanced back at her daughter. "Both of you, promise me."

It felt like someone had scrambled her insides. Bella shook her head, tears brimming. "I can't."

"Look at me," Azel said as the man called for her again. "Don't listen to him. Look at me. I can't go and face them if you aren't safe."

Aryia came to Bella's side and wrapped her hand around Bella's. "I promise, Mama."

"That's my good girl." Azel embraced Aryia before kissing her cheek. "You listen to Bella."

"I will," Aryia agreed. "Unless she is wrong."

Azel's eyes brimmed with tears as she kissed Aryia's head. "I know. I love you. Go strap in."

"Who is that?" Bella asked,

The man's voice carried to them. "Come out Azel. I know you are too stubborn to die."

"Someone trying to hurt us," Azel replied. "He killed countless people to get to me. And he will kill you and Aryia without a moment's hesitation, do you understand?"

Bella nodded. Her stomach in knots as the bile clawed its way up her throat. Why was this happening to them?

He was yelling again, but Azel ignored him as she framed Bella's face with her hands. "You take care of her. Don't let her out of your sight. I love you both." Bella nodded as tears streamed down her cheeks. They hugged, Bella holding on tightly and wishing she was braver. She wished she was strong enough to keep Azel there, but no one kept Azel anywhere she didn't want to be too long. Despite the warmth of the day, she felt chilled to the bone as Azel began to make her way across the broken corpse of their airship. Despite Azel's wishes, Bella continued to stand in the door of the hovership, watching.

That awful man was still calling out to her, but now she could see him as he paced across the gap, calling out to her with a strange cone-shaped contraption. He was tall, with dark hair cut short and fine clothing covered in blood. Men, privateers no doubt, were making their way through the ship, rifling and searching for survivors and taking loot where they could. The bodies strewn around them made Bella fear for who had been lost. For a moment, Bella lost sight of Azel. Her gut was in knots as she searched for any sign of her, making sure to stay close to the wall that kept her and Aryia from view. Just when panic was starting to set in, Azel appeared with a man beside her. Bella narrowed her eyes, trying to see who it was. When he shifted, she saw the way his hair was shaved on the side and his bulk: Draken.

Her heart swelled that he was safe. Together, they moved through the wreckage, picking across it as the bad man hauled Aleron into view. He was strapped down with metal around his upper half. His arms were cuffed, and she could see him struggling against them. Her heart sank to see her brother in such a state.

"If you don't show yourself, I'll cut him from navel to neck." The patience she'd heard in his voice earlier was gone.

"I am here," Azel called, her voice barely audible to Bella as she suddenly appeared at the edge. Azel asked a question, but Bella couldn't make out the words.

Bella strained to hear his reply. She only caught bits and pieces but determined that he was there for Azel and that her Liege would live if only she would submit. Whatever Azel's response was, it was vicious, and the man appeared concerned for the first time. His boisterous demands quieted in his throat.

"Your power will be nothing when…" The viciousness of his tone was there but the rest of the words were lost to the wind.

Before he could move, he and the guards around Aleron were suddenly lying on the ground. Others surged forward to replace them, but suddenly they, too, fell to their knees, Azel held her hands up. Though hundreds of men now knelt, Bella grew anxious. Azel was powerful and the older she became the more her abilities seemed to grow, but even she could not hold all those men that way for much longer.

Bella knew she should go, that this was the time to flee, but she couldn't look away. She needed to see Azel get to safety. A sudden movement to their left caught her attention. Draken dismounted a sand speeder long enough to haul Aleron onto the seat and then took off. As he headed toward Azel, a man wearing rags suddenly stood.

He threw his arms wide to reveal a bow with a nocked arrow. Azel focused on him, but her attempt was fruitless. The arrow flew as Draken was nearly to Azel. The speeder jerked to the side, the arrow harmlessly bouncing off its front. It took off again, with Azel stopping those who tried to pursue it.

The bow-toting man walked toward her, though the crowd of men still kneeling.

"What is he?" Aryia whispered.

Bella jumped. She hadn't even realized that Aryia had snuck out. Realizing they were in even more danger than she'd originally thought, Bella replied, "I don't know, but we have to go."

"But Mama…" Aryia's fear was plain on her face.

Azel collapsed, and the other men began getting to their feet. "Get them!" Their leader shouted. "Hunt them down and bring them back."

Draken and Aleron were gone. The man in the cloak pushed his hood back and hauled Azel to her feet. Azel slapped him. When he punched her in the gut in return, Bella covered Aryia's eyes and carried the girl to their means of escape.

Aryia wiggled free to look again. "What is he doing to mama?"

"Don't look." Bella's voice broke at the words as she took them back to the flyer.

Once they were safely strapped in, Bella adjusted the wings and wrapped her fingers around the release. Every fiber of her being wanted to stay and help Azel, but it was hopeless. Two girls without any Bloodlines against a man powerful enough to stay standing against one of the most powerful—Azel. What chance would they have? Yet, despite knowing it and despite Azel's orders, she hesitated. Fighting against the overpowering need to stay, Bella jerked the release lever down hard, and they shot off into the sand and the unknown.

Chapter 7:
"Without Water"

They were lost. Bella didn't want to admit it, but she had no idea where they were. Afraid to accidently end up circling back to the danger they'd escaped, Bella had kept moving in a single direction, but as night came, they would need to stop. Aryia napped as Bella played the events of the day over and over in her mind, wishing things had gone differently. Whenever silent tears stained her cheeks, she wiped them away, worried Aryia would awake and see them.

Endless sand stretched out before them as the soft light of a waning sun half blinded her. The rocky plateaus were still too far off, and Bella realized they weren't going to make it to them and whatever safety they might have promised. They had seemed so much closer than they actually were. A trick of the sands. To her right and left, the very tops of rocks dotted the landscape, but they were too shallow to protect them from what roamed the desert at night. Without sunlight the airship wouldn't continue to function, leaving them with very few options.

"Aryia?" Bella called as the sun touched the edge of the plateau.

The edge of the sun rested against the corner of the stone and made it appear as though the light had been cut. As it slid down to the horizon, Bella knew half of their light would be lost, but she couldn't tell Aryia that—not yet. It would only reinforce how far they were from safety.

"Aryia?" Bella said more loudly.

"What?" She sounded groggy.

"We aren't going to make it to the mountains," Bella told her. "I need you to help me search for a place high enough to set down."

Aryia shifted in her seat to sit up straighter, her neck craned. Bella split her attention between looking and piloting the ship. Finally, she spotted a triad of rocks jutting from the ground. Realizing there was little time remaining, Bella made a decision.

"I'm going to set it down, hold on."

Aryia gripped the seat as Bella positioned them toward the rocks. It wasn't much of a landing pad, but it would have to do. Without the sun, the ship's power wouldn't last long, and they couldn't risk landing in the sand. The mighty creatures that lived in it were deadly and constantly hungry.

"Hold on!" Bella called as they hit the edge of the rocks.

Reaching up, she jerked the emergency landing brake. She was immediately thrust against the straps, which dug painfully into her chest and shoulders. There was a terrible shrieking noise as the metal ground against stone. They both yelled out in fear as the ship turned sideways and tipped slightly, wedging itself against the third rock as metal groaned and something was smashed. Bella slapped her hand against the wall and ceiling in an attempt to steady herself as the ship settled. Feeling sick, Bella wiped the sweat from her forehead.

"Are you well, Aryia?" Bella called. Seeing that their energy reserves were at minimum, she flipped the switch to turn off the engine.

"Yes," Aryia replied. A quiet tinkling noise came from the engine. "Is the ship broken?"

Bella unbuckled and tried to assess the damage. They were wedged between two rocks with the third tipped them back slightly. Some of their left wing was hanging out over the sands. There was a crack in one of the windows but no broken glass. Confused about where the crashing sound had come from, she looked in the cabinet. Taking a deep breath, she slumped back.

"What is it?" Aryia asked, turning in her seat. "What broke?"

"Our water," Bella whispered, tears threatening. "Our water canisters are nearly all broken."

Aryia crawled out of her seat and hugged Bella. "We'll be fine."

Bella fought back the tears. She couldn't believe she—a grown woman—was being comforted by a six-year-old. Yet Aryia had never been a normal little girl. There was something about her that seemed to cut right into people's souls. Bella couldn't admit it aloud, but sometimes she was afraid of her niece.

"We need to figure out where we are," Aryia replied.

Bella sniffled as she nodded. "There's a map here." She reached into the compartment under the seat and extracted the thin parchment. "So we started…"

Unfurling it in the fading light, Bella set it on her lap. Squinting, she tried to orient herself. Her fingers traced over the endless sand and mountains before she found Sol. Aryia leaned in and pointed at Nova with a victorious grin on her face.

"So we were somewhere in the middle." Bella frowned, glancing between their two fingers, uncertain of where they could be.

"These look like the mountains we were headed to," Aryia whispered.

Bella tilted her head to the side to read the name. "The Rusty Range."

"No," Aryia shook her head. "They are too far away from the normal path we take between Sol and Nova. We would have had to go directly from Sol towards Momby to get there." She tapped her finger on Momby, showing how the Rusty Range sat between Sol and Momby.

Bella blinked at her, confused. "How do you know that?"

Aryia shrugged. "I like Zendar. I like to know all of its secret places."

Bella was impressed. "What if we turned toward Burtanian? Surely they would not have refused our request for aid." Bella replied. "The problem is. We don't know how long we were under attack before we crashed."

Aryia bit at her lip a little before shaking her head. "It doesn't feel right." Her finger struck the map. "What about this one?"

Pulling the map closer to her face, she read aloud, "The Hindish Mountains."

"Isn't that close to Momby?" Aryia asked, trying to crowd her head in.

Bella nodded. "Yes." Bella swallowed as she felt her stomach fall to her feet. "The city is a good three days away."

"We can't go back," Aryia replied, her voice strained with emotion. For the first time she saw tears in the young girl's eyes.

Bella gathered her niece against her as she wept. She knew the girl missed her mother, and they both feared for her fate. As darkness descended, their fear was forgotten as they cried about what had just happened.

<>

Bella woke with a start. For a moment, she didn't know what was wrong. Then she realized Aryia was holding her arm in a death grip, her eyes wide in the twin moonlights.

"What is it?" Bella asked. She licked her dry lips, wishing she could drink from the single water canister they had left.

Aryia reached over and tucked the water into their pack. "Something's coming."

"What do you mean—" The ship was jostled, as a tail slapped against the side of it, fracturing the glass. Bella fell off the seat and lay on the ground with Aryia beside her. The ship settled, but the wing was further out over the sand.

"What is it?" Bella whispered.

"Sand viper?" Aryia replied, her voice low.

They screamed as the creature struck the wing and the ship slid further along the rock. "Grab your bag," Bella yelled, fear clenching her heart in a vice. "We have to get out."

Scrambling, they gathered their rations and went for the door. The ship rocked again, and an instant later, she heard a terrible screeching noise. The ship tipped to the side as it slid off the rocks, the world turning upside down. They tumbled to the bottom of the ship. Bella's head smacked against the wall, and her vision swam. The tail slammed against the ship again, and Bella covered her head and neck as glass rained down on them.

"It's coming!" Aryia screamed, her voice sounding as panicked as Bella felt.

"Hold on!" Bella reached for her as the viper's massive row of teeth latched onto the side of their flyer like a massive sucker.

"My foot is stuck!" Aryia called out. She was wedged beneath one of the chairs. She reached down to Bella. "Take my hand!"

As Bella reached up, the snake tore at the metal, crushing it in its upper and lower jaws. Its rows of teeth swirled, ready to consume them. Foamy drool splatted the inside of the ship as Bella's fingers brushed against Aryia's. Before they could connect, the sand viper lifted the entire ship and threw it. The metal groaned as it was ripped apart.

Bella screamed as she was thrown towards the ship's nose. She tried to grip the chair, but she was thrown to the side as the ship settled. She was hanging halfway out of the ship into the dunes, Bella slowly sat up. As she slid back trying to find safety, dazed, she realized that something was rumbling. As though from a nightmare the sand viper's head rose, sand shifting off it. It started forward.

A hand clasped her shoulder, and then Aryia's other impossibly small hand shot out. A great wind seemed to appear from nowhere, and the snake was thrown back. Silence descended, the only sound their panting.

"What just happened?" Bella asked.

"We were almost eaten," Aryia replied.

Bella turned to her. "You take after your grandmother? From the Lin Bloodline?"

Aryia stared at her. "Uh…no."

"But I just saw you," Bella said, looking for her pack. "It was amazing, by the way."

"I don't have that power," Aryia replied, seemingly uncomfortable at the admission. "You do."

<>

They lay curled up on the three rocks they'd previously landed on, staying as close to the center as possible. Aryia's ankle had a nasty welt on it, and Bella found a massive lump on the side of her head, but beyond that and a few shallow cuts, they were alive and unharmed. The ship was beyond repair, so in the morning they would be walking the remaining distance to the mountain. During the day there were few predators of the sands they would have to worry about. Thankfully there were Tremblers nowhere but the Wastelands. Otherwise, they would have no chance of survival. Not that she was confident in their survival in any case when they had so little water. Zendarians could go a long time without water, but not forever.

All of that was for the tomorrow, though. For now, she dwelled on the fact that she had abilities. She had a Bloodline gift. She'd accepted long ago that she'd never have one. It happened sometimes in royal families—a relative just wasn't blessed. She'd always felt like something was wrong with her, that her inability to bear children meant that Zendar had deemed her unworthy. Before Azel, she'd questioned her worth; before Bandon, she'd lacked confidence. Sometimes, late at night, she felt like a broken useless thing. Then, when Bandon had died, she felt again that Zendar was punishing her.

Bella wiped at the tears that streamed down her face. The self-deprecating thoughts were clawing at her, wearing her down. She knew she had to be strong, but in the quiet of the midnight hour, she felt lost. If it wasn't for her promise to Azel, Bella didn't know how she'd press on. Aryia was about a quarter of her age and handling the entire situation better. Which only made Bella feel worse.

"Don't cry." Aryia's voice cut through her thoughts. "Everything will be all right."

"I didn't mean to wake you," Bella managed, kissing the top of her niece's head. "Go back to sleep."

"I love you," Aryia replied, hugging Bella's middle as she rested her head against her stomach.

Smoothing back her niece's hair, Bella whispered, "And I you."

Chapter 8:
"Unforgiving Desert"

In the morning, the sun was unrelenting. Bella loved the sun, loved the story of Zendar's love affair with Sol, but not on that day. On that day she wished for rain and clouds. Even just one cloud. Instead, the desert danced around them in a mirage of sun and sand. She knew they should stop talking, but there was something comforting about hearing Aryia's voice.

"How are you able to use my ability?" Bella asked.

"Whenever I touch someone, I can feel their gift and I can harness it," Aryia explained. "I can't explain how. Mama said I was always special and that I needed to be careful." Aryia smiled up at Bella. "But you won't be afraid of me. You're family."

Bella was a little frightened of Aryia's gift, but not of the girl. She'd always seemed strangely older than her age, more in control. Like she could see things that others couldn't. Bella remembered Azel's pregnancy with her and how strange it had been. Azel and Aleron had been incredibly secretive. Bella had thought at the time that it was because out of fear of assassins or because they were contemplating some tactical plan, but now she realized it might have been about Azel's powers. Sometimes pregnant women could act as a conduit for their baby's abilities. They hadn't acted the same way during her pregnancy with the twins, and now she knew why.

"I'll always love you," Bella replied, patting her head. "Does Aleron know?"

Aryia nodded. "He wants to keep it a secret for as long as possible. Says I don't need another reason for people to want to kill a Corvinus."

Bella's hand instinctively went to her stomach, where she'd learned the truth of those words the hard way. Age did not matter in schemes and plots. And dispatching of a child without powers was easier than killing an adult with them.

That Aleron and Azel knew exactly what their daughter was but hadn't shared it with her made her feel alienated. They were family. Why hadn't they trusted her? And then, thinking about how much

Aryia's ability truly scared her, she instantly forgave them. Often people kept secrets for good reasons.

"Your father is right," Bella replied, thought it saddened her. "Zendarians have come a long way, but they are not to be trusted. We've seen that for ourselves recently." Aryia, of course, didn't know a life before the calm that Azel and Aleron had brought to Zendar.

Aryia didn't reply, seeming to contemplate Bella's words and perhaps thinking about why they were traversing the unforgiving desert alone. Silence fell between them. Bella could have kicked herself. She hadn't meant to remind Aryia of her parents' unknown fates. The thought gnawed at Bella. Who knew what it was doing to a six-year-old's mind?

"Did your mother ever tell the story about my first meeting with Bandon?" Bella asked, peering down at the young girl's face. Her wise eyes were such a contrast to her chubby cheeks. Bella had no doubt Aryia would take after her beautiful mother. Apparently, like her mother she would have a power that struck fear in others far and wide. Thoughts for another time, perhaps.

"I remember him. He was nice," Aryia finally said.

"He was nice, but I wasn't." Bella chuckled at the memory. "Your mother is friends with the Liege of Momby, Liege Kavil. Bandon is his third son. He was always the smallest of the three of them. A few years ago he was trying to prove himself when he had his accident. His left lung had to be removed." It was like telling a story from a book she knew as intimately as her own story. "He was already sickly when I met him. I disliked him instantly and not for any reason you might think. I disliked him because he was cheerful. Because he was so happy despite what had happened to him. He was such a good person that I felt terrible about how negative I'd been about my own injury. Yet here he was, living on with a wide smile on his face." Bella found she didn't have to fight back tears, perhaps it was too dry for them to appear. "So I told him I wouldn't marry him, and I left with my nose in the air."

"Where were you injured?" Aryia asked.

"Hmm?" Bella had been so lost in her recollections that she'd only been half paying attention. "Oh." She hadn't meant to reveal that, but the damage was done. "My stomach."

Aryia reached out and gripped her hand. "Go on. What happened?" Bella smiled at her niece, who was astute enough not to apologize, only provide comfort. She was a girl far beyond her years.

"He cornered me in the garden, demanded to know why." Bella sighed at the memory. "He must have thought it was because of his disability. I refused, but he persisted until I burst into tears and told him. He was so shocked. There was a long pause, and then he left."

"He left?" Aryia replied, surprise in her voice.

"Yes." Bella nodded. "I stayed there crying until I had nothing left. I wandered around the garden until my handmaiden found me. She dressed me nicely and took me to a private dining area. There he was, smiling. As for me, I could barely meet his unrelenting stare. He asked me again to marry him. He swore that he'd spend our marriage making me happy. I fought him, but he was charming and persistent. You know the rest."

Aryia was quiet. Bella glanced at her. "What's wrong?"

"My stomach hurts." She sounded very upset.

Bella immediately started scanning for a place to rest. "Let's just make it to those rocks, and then we can have some food." She pointed.

Aryia nodded her head as they changed course. Bella could feel the same gnawing hunger and knew exactly what was in the pack. They had enough water for the day and enough food for two…maybe. They had to make it to the mountain quickly or they'd be in trouble, given how dangerous it was to travel the sands at night so far from the cities. Being close to settlements was far safer because many of the monsters had been hunted in those areas.

When they reached the rocks, they crouched against their rough, rust colored surface in relief and exhaustion. Bella was careful to split the ration so that more went to Aryia yet was cautious to conceal the difference between the amounts by holding her hand near her food as if more food—rather than emptiness—was behind it. If Aryia caught on, she would protest. As camouflage, Bella took a series of smaller bites.

"Feeling better?" Bella asked once they were done. Aryia nodded. "Good. Well, we'd better get moving." Bella held up the small metal flask that held the little water they had. "Take a sip."

"I thank you." Aryia took a swallow before passing it back.

Bella took an impossibly small drink before capping the water and putting it back in her bag. "Let's go."

Together they returned to their trek toward the mountain.

Chapter 9:
"The Mountain"

The sun was just setting as they reached the base of the mountain. Above them was an entrance to a cave toward which Bella had slowly steered them. She didn't know how they were going to get up there, but it was the first place she'd seen that might protect them from the creatures of the dunes. Glancing down at Aryia, she realized the girl was going to have a very hard time climbing.

"I'll heave you up to that first platform," Bella said, pointing at the closest natural shelf.

Aryia eyed it with a frown. "Why not just use your Bloodline to walk?"

Bella just stared. "How?" How did she even access this gift that she'd never even known she had?

Aryia shrugged. "It's within you."

"Can't you just do it?" Bella asked, offering a hand.

Aryia crossed her arms. "You have to get used to using it now that it is awake, or it will die."

Bella tapped her foot in annoyance. "Maybe this isn't the best time to practice." She gestured at the mountain.

"Now is exactly the right time," Aryia shot back, her little eyes narrowing. It was moments like this that Bella forgot she was six.

"Fine." Bella threw her hands up and turned toward the mountainside. "Fine."

Focusing on the open mouth of the cave, Bella put her hands out, imagining that wind was coming from them. Her face tensed in concentration as she willed something to happen. Her entire body was tense as she tried to push off. After a moment, Aryia burst out in laughter. Bella felt her shoulders fall as she glared at the girl.

"It isn't funny."

"It was." Aryia's eyes glistened. "Your face…" She dissolved into another round of giggles. "Priceless."

"This isn't easy," Bella replied, waving toward the cave.

"It is," Aryia replied, wiping at her eyes. "You're just trying too hard. Let it flow through you. Picture what you want, and feel it right here." Aryia touched Bella's sternum. "In your center."

"Is that how it feels for you?" Bella asked, slightly annoyed at Aryia's lecturing tone. She crossed her arms.

Aryia shook her head. "Only when I use that of others. Mine is here." She tapped the side of her head. "Like an image in my head I know what other people's Bloodlines are and I can use them but when I do I feel it here." She pressed a hand to her abdomen.

Bella groaned and closed her eyes. "I'm taking advice from a child."

"A child who can use her powers," Aryia pointed out.

Bella mock-glared at her niece's pouting face. Determined, she then faced the cave again. She imagined herself being swept up to the cave. She closed her eyes to help, trying to get the feeling, whatever it was supposed to be, to go into her. Nothing happened. With a heavy sigh, she shook her head.

"Bella, there's a creature coming," Aryia yelled, suddenly gripping her side. "Hurry! Use the wind!"

Bella's eyes popped open as fear stole all the air from her lungs. A subdued heat filled her core. Unexpectedly, she felt wind brush against her and they were half-lifted and half-thrown into the mouth of the open cave. After hitting the ground with a thud, they both moaned.

"That could have gone better." Aryia groaned again, sitting up.

"What was it?" Bella asked.

"What was what?" Aryia asked as she slowly stood, looking further into the cave.

"The creature," Bella asked, concerned it may follow them.

"There wasn't one." The smile on her face asked for forgiveness, but her eyes twinkled in triumph. It reminded her of Aleron. "My mama says Bloodlines sometimes manifest under pressure."

"You tricked me!"

Aryia's smile froze on her face. Bella felt a hand clasp around her face from behind. The heat entered her core as she screamed in fear. Wind swept away from her, driving her attacker back. She rushed to Aryia's side.

A second man, older with white streaks through his hair, helped the one who had grabbed her to his feet. Their skin was so dark that they practically disappeared into the interior of the cave. Sand People. She'd seen them in passing, but never up close and certainly never in their own territory.

"What do you want?" Bella demanded.

"You cannot be here," the older man said. "We have rights to this mountain."

"We're lost," Bella replied. "We need passage to Burtanian."

The first man, who didn't seem much older than Bella, glared. "Can you pay? We are not a charity."

Bella hadn't thought of money.

"Will you take jewelry?" Aryia burst out.

Bella glanced down in confusion. Aryia didn't have any jewelry that she knew of, and Bella only had her little Sol necklace.

"Depends on if it's real," the young man said, but the older man put a hand out.

"We shall take you before the travelers, and they shall decide." The old man turned his younger counterpart around and gestured him further in. "Go ahead and tell them."

Terrified, Bella hesitated. Aryia, on the other hand, went to take a step forward. Bella held her in place. "Can we trust them?" Bella whispered.

"Do we have another choice?" Aryia asked, glancing toward the dunes.

"No," Bella replied with a heavy sigh. "I suppose not. At least here we have a chance."

The old man lifted a lantern she hadn't noticed and turned the dial until it flared to life. "Come along, girls, or you'll get lost," he said. His frame was bent with age, and he didn't scare her as much as the younger one.

Clinging to each other, they followed the men deeper into the mountain. At first, Bella tried to keep track of all the twists and turns, but there were too many of them. As far as she could see, there were no signs or markings to give away their route. Glancing back, she realized they'd never make it back out without a guide.

"How did you come to be lost in the sands?" the old man asked.

Aryia and Bella shared a glance. They hadn't thought of what to say. Bella hesitated, but Aryia didn't. "Privateers."

The old man whistled. "They're ruthless. How did you escape?"

Bella widened her eyes and shook her head at her niece, but to no avail.

"A day ship," Aryia said.

"Where was that?" the young man asked, glancing back, looking like he wanted to go back and find it.

"A day's walk away," Bella replied before Aryia could respond. "The sand swallowed it."

The old man raised an eyebrow. "There are nearly no sand traps in this area. How unlucky that you found one."

"Unlucky indeed," Bella replied, not offering additional information and willing Aryia to do the same.

There were noises up ahead and soft light. They reached a man sitting on a stool, still and hunched like an old tree. Like magic, he seemed to come alive before their eyes, though still his bent back remained, curved with a lifetime of memories and hard labor. It was rare to see a Zendarian so old—he had to be well over a hundred years. As the three men greeted each other, Bella was overtaken by a need to squeezed Aryia's hand reassuringly.

"Yord," the sentry addressed the old man, "what have you here?"

Yord glanced back as his young associate left them to travel toward the light and sound. "Survivors, lost in the sands."

"Pamil will not be pleased." The old man's voice was coarse, though his eyes were gentle. She sensed he was trying to intimidate her, though to what end, she wasn't sure.

"Pamil hasn't been pleased since he married Melia." Yord chuckled. "Is he at the Gathering?"

Bella nearly giggled at the way his head bobbed, like his head was acting independent of his body. Were she not so terrified she likely would have laughed aloud.

"Aye, with the healer," the old man responded.

"Roland's back?" Yord asked as he waved for Bella and Aryia to follow him. "That is a surprise."

Cautiously, Bella and Aryia went to the opening. Bella took in the complex network of caves and gasped. She had heard stories about the

Sand people, but to see them herself was eye opening. For one thing, their skin was much darker than she'd expected, as though they had rolled in coals. Her own reddish skin and Aryia's golden skin were practically pale by comparison.

"You live here?" Aryia asked without judgment or prejudice, just the curiosity of a child.

Their homes appeared to be mobile, mostly tents and wagons. If the tales about the Sand people were true, these nomadic people moved from mountain to city, perhaps someone could take them to a city. Take them home. Yord waved them on, ignoring Aryia's question or perhaps not hearing it over the din in the massive cavern. They drew the attention of some, but most stayed away. When a babe waved at them, Aryia waved back, and Bella felt a smile creep on her face. Perhaps they weren't so different, these people of the sands.

When they approached a big, pale-purple tent, a woman stepped out. "Yord," the woman called with a wave. "What have you here?"

"Trespassers," Yord replied with a smile. "Devious and powerful."

Her eyes went wide in mock fear. "I can see that. Whatever are we to do?"

If only they knew, Bella thought, glancing down at Aryia. *They would not jest about such things. Thankfully only her ability had been revealed to them. Her ability, she sure liked the sound of that.*

"Is Chief Pamil available?" Yord asked, his voice taking on a more formal tone.

The woman nodded. "He's with the healer." She paused to glance at them. "You know."

When the woman went through the opening, Aryia took a step forward. Bella caught her arm. "What are you doing?" Bella asked in a hissed whisper.

"Someone's hurt," Aryia replied, her eyes unfocused. "Someone is trying to heal them. Zendar is trying to help."

Bella felt Yord's attention on them. "Aryia, not now."

"Is she of the Gift?" Yord asked, taking a step toward them. Bella pulled Aryia behind her, shielding her with her body.

"She is too young," Bella insisted, her arm squeezing Aryia's, hoping to silence the girl.

Yord's eyes narrowed. "And what about you? Was it you who is windswept?"

Aryia jerked her arm free and slipped around Bella before she could react. Calling after her, Yord followed them into the tent. Bella managed to grab hold of Aryia's shoulders just as those in the tent turned toward them in surprise.

A hefty man with his head wrapped in a maroon cloth stood. A spider web tattoo was prominent on his neck. "What is the meaning of this?" he boomed. Another man stood. His hair was short with tight curls, and he had kind eyes.

"I apologize, great Chief," Bella replied, bowing her head. "My niece was curious."

It was not the large man, Pamil, who responded but the other one—the healer. "You are familiar to me."

Fear laced through Bella, but he wasn't talking to her. His attention was on Aryia.

"You....um..." Bella tried to form words to defuse the situation, but they were stuck in her throat.

Pamil sputtered as the healer went over to them and knelt on one knee. "I know your mother. She was good to me when she did not have to be. She gave me the means to heal others." The man patted Aryia's head. "I have not seen her for some time. How is she?"

Bella was too stunned to form words. Aryia burst into tears and flung herself into the healer's arms. Puzzled, he looked up at Bella for answers.

Though her instinct told her to trust him, she did not know this man or his intentions. She said, simply, "A lot has happened."

Chapter 10:
"Old and New Friends"

Bella worried her hands and shuffled her feet as the healer carried a sleeping Aryia toward his wagon. How could she trust him when she didn't even know his name? Yet he claimed to know Azel. Perhaps Aryia had been mistaken for someone else's daughter? That was wishful thinking on Bella's part and she knew it. There was no way to be sure without asking she tried to reason but he was the first person to be truly kind to them.

His colorful wagon was bigger than she'd expected. She followed him up the short steps and into the back, where he set Aryia on the bed inside. She did not stir. How exhausted she must be! At the thought of sleep, other parts of her body reminded her of their demands, her stomach growling.

The healer glanced back at her with an amused grin. "Hungry?"

Cheeks burning she replied, "Yes."

He covered Aryia with a blanket and then rummaged around inside the wagon. She shifted from foot to foot before sitting down on a stool by an unused fire pit. He reemerged with bread, salted meat, and a persimmon, all of which he dumped into her arms.

"Eat. What is your name?" His voice was as kind as his eyes.

She hesitated only a moment. "Bella. What is yours?"

"Ah, yes. Azel spoke fondly of you. I am Rolond," he said before gesturing back to Aryia. "And she is her oldest?" Well, that settled that it, he knew Azel.

Bella nodded as she nibbled on the meat. "Aryia."

"I cannot believe how big she is." Rolond shook his head in disbelief. "Nearly Medline's age when Azel first came to us."

Bella swallowed the persimmon piece. It was old and dry but still sweet. "I do not remember you in her stories." It also meant that Roland was likely much older then he appeared.

"Did she speak of her time with the Carnival of the Sands?" Rolond asked, sitting on the wagon's bottom step.

Bella smiled and nodded. "One of her favorite stories to tell. When she was a tiger tamer." Bella felt the sadness creep in slowly, like clouds of gloom inching across the sky. "It was the twins' favorite and one of mine."

"She is my Blood sister. I carry within me the same Bloodline that gave her such strength." Rolond's voice was hushed, no doubt not wanting others to overhear. Azel and those of the Vandi Bloodline were still feared, despite what Azel had done to calm Zendar. "My power is a fraction of hers, but she never saw it that way, likely because there are so few of us left."

"I just discovered my gift. I am of the Lin Bloodline." Bella was proud that she could say such, though she could not control it yet. "I think she mentioned you. Though the Wizard Enan is always the star."

"And Aryia?" Rolond asked, his voice hopeful. "Does she take after her mother?"

Bella paused. She trusted him with who she was, but it was not fair to trust him with Aryia's secret. "She is too young. We will not know for years."

Rolond studied her face, but in the end he nodded. Bella felt a little guilty for lying, but she had to keep Aryia safe. When Bella finished the patch of meat and the old persimmon, her mouth was dry. She glanced around for a well.

"How is Azel?" Rolond asked.

Swallowing, Bella replied, "Can I have some water?"

Rolond laughed. "Not much of a healer, am I? Let me get you some." He disappeared back inside and came back with a glass bottle. He clicked the seal on the top before handing it to her. "Fresh from the ancient stream that runs deep into this mountain."

"There is water here?" Bella asked, after she'd nearly choked on her first swig of it in her haste.

Rolond nodded. "Only during a few months when the supplies at Burtanian are high. They slope off to this mountain. In a few weeks this mountain, will be dry."

Bella slowly drank some more. "Is that how you survive? Moving from place to place?"

"You mean the Sand People? Or me personally?" Rolond asked, his eyes shining.

Bella felt her face flush. "I just meant you."

"I travel in the same path, helping those that I can. I go where the water and the people are," Rolond told her, "to do what your mother bade me do all those years ago. To help bring peace and prosperity to the people of Zendar." Rolond's eyes unfocused as he stared off into the distance. "Did something happen to her?"

Bella felt her eyes prick and she tried to force the tears down. "She was taken." Her voice broke on the last word.

Rolond seemed deeply upset by the news. "By who?"

"I don't know." Her heart in her throat, she added, "They were there for her."

Rolond stood and patted her on the back. "Where do you need to go? What can I do to help?"

"Other survivors will go to Burtanian," Bella sniffled.

"Then that is where we will go." Rolond propelled her up into the wagon and told her to sleep. Curling next to Aryia, Bella drifted off, but her sleep was restless, plagued by nightmares of Azel being torn apart by dozens of hands pulling at her.

<>

Bella awoke to the jostling of the wagon. The dreams had left her feeling ill. She reached out for Aryia, but the bed behind her was empty. Panic immediately took over, and she twisted around to see the interior of wagon. The barest of light slipped in like long fingers through cracks. Dust swirled in the sunlight.

"Aryia!" Bella called out, ripping the blankets from her legs.

Suddenly a small latch to her left clicked and slid open at the front of the wagon. Blinding sunlight poured in. Temporarily disoriented, she lifted an arm against the glare. She squinted, trying to see who had stuck their head in.

"Good morning!" called Aryia's cheerful voice. "I thought you'd never wake up. You're missing all the fun."

When Aryia moved, Bella went to the space and squeezed her shoulders through. She gasped at the brilliant sunlight and the grand expanse of sand, in awe of its power. The dunes danced in the wind, catching the sunlight so they almost seemed alive with movement. Before, when they'd been running for their lives, far above the sandy mounds of their world, she hadn't been able to take in their beauty. Now that they were among the sands, Zendar was breathtaking.

"Did you sleep well?" Rolond asked to her left.

Aryia was already back in her spot on her right. Bella glanced between them; each of their heads were covered by massive hats common among the Sand People. Aryia was tinkering with some sort of box but glanced up when some landmark caught her eye.

"I rested," Bella replied, evading the question. "I didn't realize we were going to leave so quickly."

"We left at first light," Rolond told her, the reins loose in his hands. "I didn't see any reason to wake you. There is a hat inside, hanging from a nail. It's old, but it will do."

Bella nodded. She slipped back inside and sat cross-legged on the bed, trying to let her eyes readjust. Outside, Aryia asked, "Is the Wizard Enan still performing?"

"Aye, often." Rolond chuckled. "He will likely perform until his last breath."

Bella smiled. She grabbed the old hat and slid the open hatch wider so she could get her shoulders through more easily. Standing on the bench, she stared behind them. The tracks left by the wagon's skis were already being covered by the windblown sand.

She closed and latched the door tight behind her and turned to Aryia, who was leaning forward as Rolond finished his story.

"Have you ever run into bandits?" Bella asked when he was done, her eyes scanning the horizon for other life.

"Once or twice in the beginning," Rolond replied, his voice holding none of the earlier merriment. "I may not be as strong as Azel, but I am still a Vandi. They learned quickly to give me a wide berth."

Bella's gaze slid over to Aryia, who was very quiet. She was staring off into the distance with far away expression much too forlorn for her childish face. While she might be the most precocious six-year-old in all of Zendar, she was still a scared little girl whose mother had been taken.

Rolond broke the silence. "Thieves are far more common on the road. There was this one time privateers decided to attack me. They stole my Horiti, poor beasts, with the intent of leaving me to the dunes. I taught them how an old man was not to be trifled with…"

Aryia's attention returned to Rolond and his stories of hired thieves whom he'd outsmarted by making them hit each other and "trip" on air. It wasn't long until she was giggling, asking questions, and acting again like her lively self. Bella forced a smile on her face, but all the while, her mind dwelled on Azel and the hope that her brother would save her.

Chapter 11:
"Burtanian"

After camping within ruins just beyond the city, they woke at first light and quickly left. Unlike the day before, Rolond set a grueling pace for their animals. The Horiti were descendants of both camels and horses. The sun's rays made their white coats shine as their long legs pulled their wagon through the sand. Bella was still groggy as Rolond explained that they would arrive at Burtanian at nightfall. Aryia was half asleep, propped against Bella. There was an area for travelers within the Diton portion of the city where he frequently stayed.

"How well do you trust them?" Bella asked, suppressing another yawn with the back of her hand.

"Well enough," Rolond told her with a wink. "Do not worry, princess, your secret is safe with me."

Bella's cheeks burned at the comment. He was teasing her! Despite Bella's inclination to be indignant, Aryia's stifled giggle brought much needed cheer to the morning. It seemed that the old healer and young Aryia were on the verge of being friends.

"Tell me a story!" Aryia demanded in her best regal voice. That was how most of the morning was spent—listening to Rolond's stories at Aryia's behest.

"I found him strung up with a noose tight around his neck and a Horiti walking him to his death," Rolond explained, his hands gesturing to match the words. Bella could imagine "He was badly burned atop his bald head, and I'd never seen nothin' like it. He was delirious from lack of water. I cut him down, fixed him up. After a few days he woke up and told me he was a councilman in Momby."

"No!" Aryia said, her eyes fixed on his every movement.

"Yes!" he insisted. "He'd run off with his mistress only to have her steal everything and leave him for dead."

"I don't know if this is an appropriate story…" Bella said, but neither paid her any attention.

"What happened?" Aryia enthused over Bella's meager protest.

"He let me keep the Horiti," Rolond said, pointing toward the one on the right. "Itza."

Aryia and Bella burst out laughing. They hadn't expected that. Rolond, clearly quite pleased with himself, turned toward the horizon, a smile on his face. Suddenly Aryia gave an excited cry, jumped onto the bench of the wagon, and pointed to the tips of the city.

"Ah, there she is." Rolond tipped his hat back. "The walls of Diton."

As they crested the top of the dunes, the sunshine began to dip low in the sky. With trepidation, Bella asked, "Will we make it by nightfall?"

"Aye, miss." Rolond reached over and patted her on the back twice. "You need not fear. There is stone laid under the sand a good distance from the city. It keeps the bigger monsters at bay."

As she thought nervously about the distance they had yet to travel, Bella felt a soft wind against her cheek. She wished they could get there faster. Rolond seemed confident, and she wanted to trust him, but the fear was hard to push aside.

Aryia settled down next to her and elbowed her. "Cut it out."

"What?" Bella asked.

"You're leaking," Aryia told her, waving a hand down Bella's body. "You'll make the sand come up here soon."

The wind quieted. "Sorry." Bella was going to have to get used to the idea that she had a Bloodline. "I didn't mean to."

"You're new to your gift?" Rolond asked, eyeing her.

"Yes," Bella replied, bracing for criticism.

"My brother was late to his Bloodline as well," Rolond replied with a nod. "I have noticed that in some Bloodlines. Especially the Lin and the Imoten ones."

"It takes longer for them to quicken." Aryia's voice broke in.

"Quicken?" Rolond asked. "I've never heard that word used before."

"That is what Zendar calls it," Aryia replied, her voice nonchalant. Bella felt her heart clench.

Rolond raised an eyebrow in her direction, but Bella forced herself to shrug. "It's as good a word as any." She shifted under his gaze. "I actually didn't think I had a gift. I know it is rare that anyone in their twentieth year or later gain an ability."

He did not press the issue. "Aye, my brother was in his nineteenth year. He worried the same until his skin slowly hardened."

"Are you close with your brother?" Aryia asked. "I'm close with mine, although they are very loud."

Rolond chuckled. "We were. He died some years back in a rockslide."

"I'm so sorry to hear that," Bella replied, touching his shoulder in sympathy. "May Zendar watch over his soul."

Rolond nodded to her in appreciation. "There is the entrance." He gestured to their left.

A row of wagons and a few flying machines were outside the gates. The view troubled Bella. "Why aren't they getting in?"

"They either can't pay or don't have an authorized location." Rolond patted Aryia's head as she yawned. "I do. No need to worry. If the guards give us trouble, I have coin enough to pay."

Despite his assurances, they passed the next few minutes in silence as the walls drew closer. Bella searched the faces of those close by and saw no one she knew. Even if they were survivors from the crash, she wouldn't know everyone on the ship. In vain, she searched for what she wanted to see—the one face that mattered, though she knew it wouldn't be there.

Aryia slumped against her, curling in her lap as they drew closer. The comfortable stillness was broken as they reached the gate. A man was arguing with the guards, yelling as he shoved at one of them. His companion began shouting obscenities, and Aryia suddenly clung to Bella's waist.

Looking to their guide, Bella asked, "Is there another way in?"

Rolond immediately shoved the small slat open. "Best get inside. Stay quiet."

Bella shoved Aryia into the opening before sliding in feet first. Once they were inside, Rolond closed and latched it. They were plunged into darkness with only the barest of moonlight winking through the cracks. They clung to each other, listening to the muffled sounds of sword fighting.

A sudden wind current started within the wagon. "Is that me or you?" Bella asked, trying to calm down.

"I don't know," Aryia whispered, the words muffled against Bella's chest.

She suppressed her fear, and the wind quieted. Suddenly, they heard Rolond's voice. It sounded like he had jumped down from the carriage, and Bella strained to make out the words. There was some more shouting, and then all went quiet. Fear roiled in Bella's stomach, and she felt lightheaded as the realization that Rolond might not come back settled in. A minute ticked by, and then two, eons of muffled confusion filling her mind.

The slat opened, startling them both. "We're good," Rolond called, "but you best stay in there."

He slid the door closed before she could answer. The wagon lurched forward, and Bella almost fell backward. Relief flooded through her as Aryia detangled herself from Bella's hold.

"I want to see," Aryia called from the darkness. The small door slid open.

"You should stay inside," Rolond whispered.

"I'll stay inside," Aryia insisted, her face pressed against the narrow opening. "I just want to see."

Rolond sighed. "You can see, but the first sign of trouble, you'll go back inside. Agreed?"

"Agreed."

Bella collapsed on the mattress with a sigh. Aryia was going to be the death of her! After a minute, though, she joined Aryia, her face pressed against the opening above her niece's. The city was filled with pale yellow lights that lined windows. It was a quiet street with old buildings made of stone—some pale, some yellow, and some red. Together, they created a smear of color, punctuated by the moonlit areas washed of it.

After a few minutes, they left the sleepy side of the city and entered a lively area. A woman was singing from a balcony with not enough clothes on, and two men were arguing in the street. Up ahead she could hear the beating of the drums and rowdy laughter. A block up from there, ladies dressed in provocative clothing called out to Rolond. Bella covered Aryia's face, to her protest.

Once they were out of view, Bella let Aryia watch again. From there on out there were a few establishments open, a few restaurants and inns. Some houses were still lit up, but most were not. Despite the fact that people slept within them, the area felt somehow deserted. Void of life and sound. Something about it was unnerving.

When they reached a gate, Rolond murmured, "Stay here." He vanished, although they could hear him off to the left. Minutes ticked by before he returned. "All clear." The gate swung open, and they were admitted. Aryia yawned again.

"I'm ready to sleep," she whispered. Aryia shifted away to get comfortable on the bed. Apparently now that the excitement was over, so was she.

When the wagon came to a stop, Rolond leaned back. "Best get some sleep. I'll keep everything locked up tight."

"Where will you sleep?" Bella asked, afraid to be left alone.

"Don't worry about me. Tabitha always has spare beds." Rolond smiled, his white teeth stark against the dark and shadowed features of his face. "You're perfectly safe. We'll talk more in the morning."

Chapter 12:
"Whispers of Home"

Bella woke to the annoying call of an animal. She'd heard of such creatures that rose with the dawn, but never seen them herself. She'd read these low flying birds loved Diton, which boasted a few small parks in its inner and outer walls. They lived on the berries that grew on the trees. The first harvest of those berries could be eaten by people, as they were sweet and succulent. The second and third batches—before the heat forced them to hibernate and the cycle began again—always tasted like raw meat. So they were left to the birds, who had no such issue with their flavor. Part of her was excited to see one, but Roland's last instruction to stay where they were outweighed her curiosity.

"What is it?" Aryia asked, her voice muffled. Light streamed into the wagon through narrow slats where the boards didn't quite meet.

"A bird," Bella replied, rolling over. She was still tired, as it had taken her some time to ignore the subdued sounds of the city. Exhaustion had finally won out, but her night had not been restful.

"Make it stop," Aryia replied with a groan.

Bella sat up, light shining across her feet. What harm could a little peak outside do? She crept to the door and unlatched it. Slowly, it swung open. Popping her head outside, she could see other carriages and flying machines. Some had people around them, but she didn't recognize anyone. The fresh air and sweet aroma of nearby cooking tempted her. Vacillating between going fully out and staying in, she pulled the door closed, not ready to leave Aryia. She crawled back next to her niece and cradled Aryia against her. The scent of herbs from the bedding encircled them, and the girl sighed contentedly.

"I'm happy you're with me," Aryia whispered.

Bella kissed the top of her head. "I'm happy *you're* with me." Aryia giggled before snuggling closer, a strong contrast to her normally adult-like behavior.

There was a long pause. "I wish my mama and papa were here."

“Azel would be happy to see Rolond again,” Bella replied absentmindedly. “But there isn’t enough room on this bed for them and us.”

Aryia burst into laughter. “This bed isn’t big enough for just Papa!”

“Could you imagine Aleron trying to squeeze into this wagon?” Bella laughed so hard that her abdomen hurt and tears sprang to her eyes. They would have continued on in the same fashion if there hadn’t been a knock on the door.

Bella sat up, instinctively shielding Aryia with her body. “Good morning!” Rolond called out, and Bella instantly relaxed. “Breakfast is ready when you’re ready to come out.”

Aryia climbed over Bella as she shouted, “I’m hungry now!”

Chuckling, Bella fixed her dress. Her clothes felt stale and dirty, but what was she to do? No change of clothing and no chance for a bath. Slightly embarrassed by her state, Bella was not enthusiastic to leave the safety of the wagon. But when Aryia practically flew out of it, Bella reluctantly followed.

They drew the stares of others in the courtyard, but Bella focused on the house. It was quaint, small even, but had a sprawling courtyard that reminded her of the palace gardens on Sol with its intricate placement of stone and trees. From the trees wind chimes dangled like earrings. They sang with each burst of Zendar’s exhalations, drawing her eye. Mirrored decorations also hung from the branches of trees, swinging wildly in the breeze.

They entered the house to sounds of merriment in a massive room to their right. It was more like a tavern than a family dining room. Men and women were eating a banquet of morning bread and pastries. She could smell eggs and some sort of steaming meat. Aryia floated toward the aromas as Bella realized how much she missed fresh food.

Glancing at Rolond she asked, “Can we?”

“The meal is included.” He smiled, waving them forward, and trailed behind them. People called greetings to Rolond, but few paid her or Aryia any mind

A portly woman with colorful skirts and a mop of black hair entered the room, carrying in a pitcher of juice. Bella filled a plate, helping Aryia with hers before taking a seat. Before Rolond could join them, the woman pushed her way through the crowd toward them.

"Aye, you must be the mountain girls," the woman said with a broad smile. "Not often does Rolond take in strays. Let me get a look at you." She reached over and tilted Aryia's head back by her chin. "Pretty little thing, ain't cha? Your family must be from the Undel region with such honey-touched skin." She turned a critical eye on Bella, her fists on her hips. "You look right. All skin and bones. You from this region?"

"Yes!" Bella squeaked.

The woman chortled at her response and slapped her leg in good cheer. "Are you of the mountain or of mice?" People close by jeered.

"Tabitha"—Rolond put a hand on her shoulder—"these girls have been through quite enough without your heckling."

"I don't mean nothin' by it," she said, her general jovialness unchanged.

Rolond patted her shoulder. "You never do." He took a seat next to Bella, crowding in close. "But these girls paid for anonymity along with safe passage, and you know how serious I am about that."

Tabitha glanced between them before leaning toward Bella. "If you're running from a wicked husband, there is plenty of work for good girls and their daughters." Tabitha winked before moving off.

Bella's mouth dropped open in shock as she glanced at Aryia, who was picking at her meal and doing a poor job of hiding her smirk. Rolond was suddenly very fascinated by his food as well. Bella was utterly at a loss for words.

"We are not telling Azel or my brother this part of the story," Bella murmured before digging into her food.

"I do have bad news," Rolond said some minutes later after most of their plates were clean.

Bella stilled. "Oh?" She tried not to sound as panicked as she felt.

"There is war on everyone's lips. News of the Liege Corvinus's injury and Queen Azel's kidnapping has spread like a sandstorm. Apparently the Liege Corvinus has been seen amassing an army to save his missing queen," Rolond told them, his voice hushed. "Burtanian is preparing to close its gates until the fighting has passed. If I am to continue on my route, I must leave today before the evening guard."

"Where will we go?" Bella asked, her fingers wrapping around Aryia's wrist.

"There is an inn within the edge of Burtanian where you will be safer," Rolond told her. "There is talk of a man searching for survivors within the inner walls, but the owner of the inn is an old friend. It is best that you go there."

Aryia sat up straighter. "We should go." She was addressing Bella with that now-familiar oddly mature expression, as though she knew something Bella was not privy to.

Unnerved but unwilling to show it, Bella nodded. "I agree that would be best. We don't want to be more of a hindrance than we already have been."

Rolond shook his head. "You have been a delight, but I have people waiting for the supplies I'll carry from Tabitha."

"We understand." Aryia's grin could have melted iron—it was pure sunshine.

"We do?" Bella asked and then saw Rolond's relieved expression. "I mean, we *do*."

He patted Aryia's head. "I'll get you settled before I leave. Don't worry, girls. Your trials are nearly over."

Despite his intent, the words brought Bella no comfort.

Chapter 13:
"Elbow Grease"

Bella sighed in boredom from where she lay on the bed. How many times could she count the lines of sunlight that poured through the inn's slatted windows? Aryia was reading beside her from a book the innkeeper had, one for younger children. From the looks of it, the distraction wouldn't last the night. At home, Bella had had many duties to perform, from charitable work to taking care of her nieces and nephews. Here she felt helpless and useless.

Sitting up, she glanced at Aryia. "I'll see if the innkeeper needs help." She couldn't stay still any longer. Plus, Rolond had told her that the innkeeper would be happy to lessen her nightly pay if she contributed in some way. She wasn't sure what that entailed, but she had to be able to help with *something*.

To Bella's surprise, Aryia snapped the book closed and stood. "I'll join you."

"There's no reason. You can stay here."

Barely were the words out of her mouth before Aryia was shaking her head. "I want to."

Perhaps it would be best if they stayed together. Even if in a place that seemed safe, there were no guarantees. She touched her stomach, memories of assassins attacking her in the palace resurfacing.

Bella shrugged. "Four hands are better than two."

They found the innkeeper's wife and daughter-by-marriage behind the bar in the tavern. Though it was early in the day, it was already starting to fill up. The innkeeper's son was in the corner with a game of Hak-Ta, watching closely where two boards were going simultaneously. There were two boards going at the same time, where the son was watching closely. They wandered up to the counter, and Bella lifted Aryia onto the stool.

"Mistress Bella"—the innkeeper's thin wife drew closer to them—"what brings you here? Ready for lunch already?"

"Mistress Zoya, you said earlier there might be work," Bella said.

Her eyes brightened. "Yes! I have dishes that need cleaning. Follow me." She waved them around the bar, raising a section for them to get through before walking them into a kitchen.

The room was hot, with a young man tending to a fire and an old woman stooped over a stove. They exited out a knobless door to the left that swung easily on its hinges. The smell of cooking food was quickly replaced with that of animals. It was not a pleasant smell, and Bella had to force herself not cover her nose. A small house sat in front of her with a smattering of large funny-looking birds—their feathers a smattering of black, white, and brown. When Zoya strode past them, they made a strange gobbling noise that caused Aryia to giggle.

There were small raised garden beds and some larger animal pens further out, including one holding large cattle. All of it was surrounded by a sturdy stone wall. Beyond that she could see buildings rising and the massive inner wall of the city. When they rounded the corner, she saw a pile of pots and other dishes under the outer kitchen window. A young boy was scrubbing at a pot with a metal brush; his head bent but she guessed he was a few years older than Aryia. Bella could hear its metal bristles scraping.

"Oye, Mel," Zoya called.

The young boy groaned. "Whatcha want, Ma?" he called back, his entire focus on pot. "Can't you see I'm busy?" His voice was a whine.

Zoya whopped him across the back of the head. "Don't you sass me, boy." The pot fell to the ground and the boy covered the back of his head with his hands. "Especially since I brought you two helpers."

When the boy finally noticed them, his eyes opened wide. Instantly he stood to attention, a blush across his cheeks. He stammered, trying to form words as everyone leaned forward trying to decipher what he was saying. He reminded Bella of what happened at home when most people of their city met royalty for the first time.

"Spit it out, Mel." Zoya put her hands on her hips. "You're embarrassing yourself."

That only deepened the red of his cheeks, and he averted his gaze in shame. Unsettled by Zoya's coarse behavior toward her son, Bella smiled warmly, trying to reassure him. "I'm Bella, and this is my niece, Aryia. Your name is Mel?"

He nodded as his mother sighed. "Get them all cleaned by the end of the day, and you earned three square meals." Without any other instructions, Zoya left, returning to her bar, no doubt.

"Do you have another one of those?" Aryia asked, pointing to the brush.

"You can use this one." He thrust it toward them. "It's new."

Aryia shyly smiled as she took the brush. She reached out and took a pot before sitting down, unceremoniously, in the dirt. The boy glanced at Bella and then Aryia before jumping up and patting the stool.

"You can have this," he told Bella. "I'll get us more brushes."

Before she could respond, he darted to the end of the building and inside. Aryia giggled. "I like him."

"You like everyone," Bella replied as she sat on the stool and eyed the dozen or so pots and pans. "This is going to take a while."

Aryia shrugged. "We don't have anything else to do, and three meals sound delicious."

When Mel returned, he showed them how to properly clean the pots using the brushes and sand to scrape off the worst of what was stuck to the bottoms. After a while, Bella fell into a routine, her mind tracking the day's passage with the position of the sun. Aside from the break they took for lunch, they worked steadily, her focus on the task at hand keeping her distracted from darker thoughts, such as war and Azel's fate. Before she knew it, night had come.

Aryia yawned as Bella set her last pot down. "That's all?" Bella asked, pleased that there were no more.

During the course of the day a few more had been added, but still they had been able to finish them. Bella stood and stretched, her spine and back muscles protesting the single position she'd held for the last hour. Aryia, who had been helping Mel with his last pot, smiled at Bella. There was a smudge of black on her face.

"I think it's time for a bath," Bella told her with a smile. "Where are the closest baths?" she asked Mel.

He didn't hesitate, no longer intimidated by them. "It's a good few blocks from here. My sister goes about this time. She can take you."

He rocketed to his feet and was off before they could respond. He had a tendency of doing that, Bella had noticed. Though she'd seen

Zoya roll her eyes when he did, Mel probably didn't know how fondly his mother looked at him when he wasn't paying attention. Until she'd seen that during one of their meals, Zoya's behavior had been upsetting. Janvi, Mel's sister-by-marriage, held no such kindness for the boy. Bella was a little worried about how the woman would react to Mel getting her for them.

Aryia covered her mouth, trying to stifle a yawn as Bella began walking toward the house with the last two pots in her hands. Thankfully, these were much smaller than some of the others. Her arms were sore and she was anticipating the comfort of a bath. She imagined letting the warm waters loosen her muscles at a bathhouse or whatever hot room they had. Not to mention her aching fingers.

Aryia trailed behind her, rubbing at her eyes. It was moments like this that Bella realized how young she was, this a constant contradiction of precociousness and childish sweetness.

Mel came barreling out of the door. Bella stumbled backward, dropping one of the pots as she back-pedaled before falling squarely on her bottom in the dry earth.

"Mel!" his sister-by-marriage scolded him, holding the door open. "Go help her up!"

"Sorry, Janvi! Sorry, Bella!" Mel rushed to take the pot from the ground before bolting back to the kitchen.

Aryia helped her up as Janvi shook her head. "That boy is a menace." Janvi's tone was harsh.

Bella smiled, trying to defuse the situation. "He certainly has a lot of energy."

Janvi eyed her for a moment, seeming to look down her nose at them. "Get your things. I'll be heading to the bath shortly."

Bella ushered Aryia inside, waving to Mel as they hurried past. Not thrilled with Janvi's attitude, but not willing to incur her wrath, Bella rushed to gather the clothes and few cleaning items they had. They'd need to buy oil, but most bathing areas had it in stock. At least the finer baths did—she'd never been to an establishment like the one they were going to. Aryia was all yawns, and Bella practically carried her down the stairs. They found Janvi leaning on the corner, talking to Mel's mother, when Bella turned the corner. Unlike earlier, the tavern was packed. Bella immediately put Aryia in front of her, afraid to let go of her shoulders. Together they weaved through the crowd to Janvi.

"We're ready." Bella told her when she'd finally pressed her way through the thong of people.

"About time," Janvi said with a roll of her eyes. Turning to follow, Bella was startled when a hand grasped her arm.

"Look at this pretty thing." Bella cringed. The man was older, his hair thinning on top of his head. His breath smelled of cheap libations.

"Let me go," Bella said, jerking back and bumping into another man.

Air suddenly brushed against her cheek, a wind picking up. Still holding her arm, the man began looking around him. Bella tried to stop, tried to quiet her ability, but it was building with her fear. Aryia tugged on Bella's hand and said something to her, but the words were lost to the crowd.

"Who is of the Bloodline?" she heard someone close to them ask.

Something slammed against the counter. Zoya glared at the men. "Let her go."

Just like that, she was free and rushing after Janvi, who had abandoned them. Bella sent a thankful glance back to Zoya, who was watching her under a scrupulous eye. Undoubtedly, Zoya would be asking her later to explain. Powers were growing increasingly rare. Fewer people were born with abilities each year.

When they emerged from the building, Janvi was standing with her hands on her hips, talking to a very large girl.

"About time," Janvi snapped, her gaze as severe as her words. "Try not to keep me waiting."

Bella gritted her teeth, knowing she was in no position to set her straight and knowing that she couldn't—*shouldn't*. Janvi reminded her of the concubines that Aleron had had before Azel had come. They had been cruel and manipulative to her as a child. The thought of Azel, who had changed so much in Bella's life and had shown Bella so much care, reminded her of how lucky she really was. Straightening her spine, she faced Janvi fully.

"Which way?" Bella asked, meeting her gaze straight on.

Janvi only glared in response before huffing, tossing her long dark brown hair over her shoulder, and strutting down the street. She wondered how quickly Janvi's attitude would change if she knew she was in the presence of two princesses. Bella glanced at Aryia, who shrugged.

Aryia's once tired eyes flashing with cunning. "She'll learn the hard way."

Chapter 14:
"Prejudice"

Bella held the collar of the thin robe up to her throat with her right hand as she stood in the doorway of the bathhouse. For some reason she felt so exposed among these strangers. She had taken her time undressing, not wanting to be stuck with Janvi too long. Women of all sizes and shapes were dispersed around the hot room, lounging in pool and sitting on colorful stone benches. She'd never seen so many nude people before. Children sat in a smaller pool, some splashing but all surprisingly well behaved.

Aryia eyed them. Bella could see her gears turning. "You can go play."

Aryia shook her head and tightened her hold on Bella's two smallest fingers.

"I'll go with you," Aryia told her.

Bella shuffled toward one of the less-used pools, furthest from the wall where the steam came from. Quickly, setting the small rented basket to the side of the bathing area, Bella went to a nearby bench. Steadying herself, she untied her robe and set it down before wading into the water. Bella retrieved the soap from the basket to begin cleaning the grime from herself and Aryia. An older woman, well into her hundreds, was speaking quietly to a younger woman when Aryia and Bella joined them.

"Blessed day," Bella managed with a smile as she settled into the cool water. Her skin immediately broke out into a prickle of raised hairs at the sudden chill.

"Praise be to Zendar," the older woman replied, barely stopping her conversation.

Aryia joined her, and they sunk up to their chins. Dipping her head back, Bella let her eyes close. She'd missed her baths. They were traditionally a time for Azel and Bella to spend with the children. Soon, though, the twins would be too big to join the women. By then, Bella had hoped to have another niece to spoil. She swallowed hard as she sat up, her mind reeling from thoughts of Azel. Her chest tightened as she fought back tears. Determined to stay busy, she helped Aryia bathe, using the scrubbing stones and running a bone-toothed comb though her hair.

"She your daughter?" one of the women asked.

Bella blinked and glanced at them. The older woman's face was wrinkled like a prune. "She's my niece."

The elder grinned broadly as she turned to the other woman. "I told you she wasn't old enough. Such young dears all alone. Breaks my heart." The older woman sniffled as the other woman patted her shoulder.

"Do you have family?" the younger woman asked.

"We're trying to get home," Aryia told them before Bella could speak.

"And I'm older than I look," Bella replied, realizing that with her slight curves and childish face she must seem years younger to them. "I've been married."

"Look at me, making assumptions on age! Insulting you." The older woman chortled. "The older you get, the less you can recognize age. You could be forty for all I know." She continued laughing as though she'd made some great joke.

Bella was uncomfortable. She had never been very good around strangers—too many of them had tried to kill her. Plus, she'd never had to mingle in such informal settings as a bath. As a princess, she was accustomed to people keeping their distance.

"How old are you?" Aryia asked, her eyes seeming to bore into the old woman. Clearly, she had no such issues about socializing. "You must be over a hundred with all those wrinkles."

The two women looked at each other in stunned silence. Bella was utterly shocked by Aryia's bluntness. She'd never seen her so crass. As Bella was about to censure her, the two women burst out laughing. One slapped the water as she hooted. They were drawing attention to their corner of the baths, but Aryia didn't seem to care.

"Indeed, I am over that dreadful mark." The old woman wiped tears from her cheeks. "It isn't just my skin but my bones that know old is old."

"Aryia," Bella said softly. "We should finish up and go."

"No need to rush," the older woman said with a reassuring smile. "The baths are the only place we're guaranteed time away from the men."

"We've just had a long day," Bella replied, suddenly ready to be anywhere else.

Almost on cue, Aryia yawned, her head bobbing in agreement. She waved farewell as they put on their robes. They found Janvi and her large friend laughing with a group of women.

Janvi frowned as they approached. "It's the mountain girl," she sniggered.

Bella froze in surprise, finally understanding why Janvi didn't like them. Janvi was prejudiced against the Sand People and had mistakenly assumed Bella was one. The other women jeered at her, and Bella felt her face burn in mortification. Tears pricked her eyes as she felt everyone in the bath was watching her. She tightened her hold on Aryia's hand. Wind pressed against her legs as her emotions rose.

"You'll regret that!" Aryia shouted, stepping forward.

Bella shook her head, pulling Aryia close to her. "They're just people, like you or me," Bella said to Janvi as she thought of Roland's kindness. "I've seen more kindness from them than exists in your little finger. You have a lot to learn!"

Janvi gaped in surprise. The other women heckled Janvi without hestiation, turning on her in an instant. Her face flushed with anger as Bella retreated. She went to the desk and gave them the token and the basket. The attendant returned their items and they hurried to the dressing rooms to change. Afraid of what Janvi would do, Bella rushed to dress her and Aryia, not even bothering to bind either of their hair properly, just half braiding.

"I want to go home," Aryia whispered, as they exited with Aryia clinging to her skirts.

Kneeling down, she took Aryia's hands. "We'll find a way home soon. Someone is bound to be looking for us."

Aryia nodded, fat tears in her eyes. Bella kissed her head before standing to lead them home. Thankfully, they were only a few short blocks from the inn. The streets were surprisingly busy for the time of night, but most people were in front of their houses—adults talking and children playing.

Bella repeated Janvi's words in her mind again and again, trying to determine the best step forward. She didn't doubt that Janvi would continue to discriminate against her. Even if she wasn't one, Bella couldn't stand to stay in that inn any longer. Janvi had accomplished her mission—she was going to leave. Bella wondered if there was a place nearby.

Suddenly, Aryia's hand slipped away. Bella immediately turned back and saw her watching a group of men who were walking down the street. As Bella went grab her, a group of women strode past between them. By the time Bella managed to push through them, her heart hammering in her chest, Aryia was turning the corner.

"Aryia!" Bella called, not sure what her niece was thinking. "Come back!"

Bella rushed after her and nearly froze as she, too, turned the corner and saw the men Aryia had followed. They were dressed like warriors. They reminded her of Drake and were, no doubt, just as deadly.

"You shouldn't wander off!" Bella said, taking Aryia's arm.

"Don't worry," the biggest warrior called, waving sweetly to them. "We're not as scary as we look."

One man punched him. "You're being weird," the tallest said as the others cackled.

"She's my daughter's age," the big one said with a shrug before they continued on their way.

Bella glanced down at Aryia, wondering if she had sensed they weren't a threat. Bella wouldn't put it past her. In a way, Bella had just judged them on how they looked, like Janvi had done for what she'd assumed they were. It was harder not to judge than she'd first thought.

"They were telling me about…" Aryia paused. "About the Liege Aleron's general. He's apparently looking for refugees." Her gaze was unfocused.

As they reached the edge of the street Bella stopped. Draken. "Really?" Bella scanned the thoroughfare as though expecting him to appear. "Draken's here?" Hope swelled within Bella's breast.

Aryia shrugged. "Somewhere."

As they passed an alleyway, a hand shot out from the darkness and grabbed hold of Bella's arm. She gasped as it jerked her violently into the darkness. She landed hard in the dirt a moment before Aryia joined her. Shocked, Bella blinked, rolling onto her stomach she tried to catch her breath. A pair of boots appeared next to her head and then a second pair.

"What do we have here?" a rough male voice asked.

Bella opened her mouth and let out a scream before a foot connected with her side. All the air went out of her. As she struggled to scream again, she felt an arm wrap around her. A hand clamped over her face as she was carried deeper into the darkness. The smell of straw and manure filled her senses—a stable.

Tears ran freely down her cheeks, unchecked. She struggled when she saw the empty Horiti stall, panic rising up within her. They were going to assault her. The idea of being violated suddenly brought life back to her. She opened her mouth and bit down—hard. The man yelled and dropped her as she rushed away.

"Help!" she screamed an instant before a hand connected with the side of her face.

Chapter 15:
"Taken"

Bella tasted blood in her mouth, the metallic tang odd and surreal, as she heard the sound of fabric tearing. It took her a moment to realize it was her clothing. Memories cascaded in as she immediately started to kick and push away from the man. He held her ankles in place, spread apart, and cursed at her as he leaned over her. The smell of booze wafted her way.

"Let me go," she moaned, her head throbbing. He ignored her pleas as he trapped her legs and started fumbling with his pants.

Suddenly, Bella felt power flow through her. The wind began to pick up. He paused what he was doing and glanced around, his mouth hanging open in shock. She couldn't focus as the wind began to howl. It whipped wildly around her, and she began to lift off the ground. The man called out, jumping back from her. Almost instantly there were two more men there yelling at each other. The Horiti started to shuffle around their stalls. The doors and shutters began to shake.

Anger, shame, hatred, and disgust swirled within her. She wanted them to suffer, but more than that—more than *anything*—she wanted them to go away. Lifting a hand caused a sudden fluctuation in the room, a force slamming against the man who had touched her, who had wanted to defile her. Her focus narrowed as she lifted him off the ground and begin extracting all the air from his body. Detached from herself, she saw him struggling to breathe, saw him clawing at this throat. But she didn't care that he was suffering—she was beyond caring.

As she continued to hold her attacker in place, one of the other men shouted, getting her attention. He held up Aryia, whose eyes were wide with fear, and pressed a knife to her throat.

All of the fight went out of Bella. She dropped to her feet before collapsing to her knees. Her whole body was shaking, and she could barely focus. Her teeth chattered, though she wasn't cold.

Her eyes never wavered from the knife as Aryia reached up and touched the man's wrist. He grunted, dropping the blade and stumbling back. The other man yelling to him as Bella reached for the stall opening, trying to get to her feet. Sand suddenly filled the room, washing like a wave over the men. Aryia landed on her feet before falling forward and catching herself on her hands.

Pushing herself up, she rushed towards Bella, who opened her arms. "I stopped him," Aryia exclaimed, her voice muffled against Bella's neck. "I took away Zendar's gift."

Bella didn't have the energy to dwell on the fact that apparently Aryia could not only use other's gifts but also remove whatever Bloodline gift they had. That was a problem for future Bella, present Bella had more pressing issues.

"You were brave," Bella managed. "We have to go." She stood and staggered toward the second door, using Aryia has a crutch. Her only focus was to get them as far away as she could.

She unlatched the door. The moment she shouldered it open, someone grabbed onto her hair from behind. She shrieked in pain as she was yanked backwards. Aryia turned back to her, and Bella yelled, "Run!"

Bella felt herself slammed against the side of a stall. The Horiti inside reacted violently, honking in surprise as it kicked at its door. All the animals were agitated, their calls of distress filling the air. One of the other men called out that they all should flee, but the man who towered over her refused.

"Aryia, run!" Bella called weakly as her niece hesitated. Suddenly, a man appeared behind Aryia and wrapped her in a sack. Bella screamed and dashed toward the door, following the man, who picked up Aryia like a satchel of food and carried her under his arm as he jumped into a wagon.

The man kicked the door closed, and just like that Aryia was gone. Bella felt a hand wrap around her waist. She brought her elbow up and connected with his head. He shoved her forward, and she crashed headfirst into the partition. Dazed, she slumped against the wall, her head throbbing.

He called her a series of slurs as he jerked her back. Clothing ripped as he tore at her and she weakly fought him, feebly calling for Aryia. As quickly as his attack started, though, it abruptly ended. Her head lolling, she felt blood splatter against her. The man fell hard to the ground as another stood over him.

Blinking the haze from her eyes, she tried to see the face of the new man. He was massive, easily thrice her size. When he reached for her, she softly protested. It was enough to make him hesitate as he crouched beside her.

"Bella, it's me." Draken's voice broke through the fog in her mind.

"Drake?" she asked, leaning toward him to catch sight of his face before she launched herself into his arms. She burst into tears as she clung to him, a wave of relief washing over her. It was over! And then she remembered. "They have Aryia."

"Who does?" Draken stood, supporting her easily with one arm.

"The door." Bella pointed, trying weakly to reach the latch.

They were through the door in an instant, but the side street was nearly deserted. Bella wiped her nose and winced. She saw blood on her hand and her head ached like someone had it in a vice. Clinging to him to stay upright, she pointed in the direction the wagon was traveling.

"We have to find her." She took two steps before her legs began to wobble. Draken caught her before she could collapse. He carried her to the edge of the street before searching both ways. "There was a wagon!"

"It's gone," Draken replied, turning his attention back to her. "And you're in no position to assist."

Helplessness swamped her, making her feel constricted. Tears muddled her vision as she clung to Draken. Together they made their way through side streets and narrow alleys. Time was all over the place; Bella couldn't keep track as her thoughts sloshed around her head. Part of her wanted to cry out that they were going away from Aryia, but most of her just wanted to rest.

When they reached a building, Draken strode toward one of the rooms. A woman called to him as Bella felt him lift her up. It reminded her of the day the world had shaken. His heady scent filled her senses as she drifted.

With a start, she opened her eyes when he set her down. "We have to help her," Bella managed, trying to sit up.

"I'll go back," Draken insisted. "You need to rest."

"Find her," Bella managed, her body demanding sleep as her mind struggled to stay awake. "Find Aryia."

Draken leaned close. "I will look for her. If you need anything, Vyoma is the proprietor of this inn."

Bella snagged his hand and forced her eyes wide as sleep tugged at her. Her mouth felt furry as she focused on Draken. "Come back." The words barely were past her lips before she collapsed into oblivion.

Chapter 16:
"Tender Brutality"

It felt like a herd of Horiti had trampled on her head. Trying to blink the sleep from her eyes, she slipped the sheet off. When she yawned, her lip protested, and she hissed in pain. Squinting, she scanned the room for water. The thought immediately made her bladder wake up and also demand attention. It was eerily quiet for the middle of the day. There were some sounds, but they were far off. Pulling the door open a crack, she peered into the adjoining room. It was a circular indoor courtyard with a dry fountain, and every color of stone made up intricate designs. Shifting from foot to foot, she scanned the doors until she saw one marked with the sun and the other with Zendar—indicating male and female.

Shuffling toward the one with the sandy world of Sol carved into the wood, she prepared for the worst. Outside of the palaces, indoor plumbing was limited to the bathhouses and steam rooms. Surprisingly, however, the smell wasn't bad, indicating it was well maintained. The hole in the floor made her sigh, but nature would have her way.

Once her business was completed, she went in search of water. The light of the sun poured through two massive windows on each side. Curtains kept most of the bugs away, a stale breeze making them dance.

"Who are you?" a woman's voice asked.

Bella yipped in surprise as she jumped to her left. Her head throbbed, and her body protested at the sudden movement. She turned to see a woman wearing a stern expression. When their eyes met, her expression shifted to confusion and then concern.

"Who did that to you?" She set down the two pails.

"I…" Bella tried to form words, but her mind was drawing a blank. "There were…"

"Bella?" Draken's voice caught her attention. "Good, you're up."

The other woman forgotten, she turned to Draken. He closed the front door behind him as he came toward her. His expression was strained, and she could see the edge of exhaustion in his features. Had he been searching for Aryia all night?

"Any news?" Bella asked, hopeful.

"No. I have people searching for her," Draken replied, his eyes on the other woman. "She's my guest."

A shadow of contempt marred the woman's face. "Did you do that to her?"

Bella gasped. "He would never!"

At the exact same time he curtly said, "No."

The woman's eyebrows rose as her eyes darted between them. "I don't want to know, but you don't look married, so my rules still apply. You'll have to book a second room."

"Of course, Vyoma," Draken replied, hunting for a coin from the pouch on his hip. "Here's for another night for me and a night for the room next to mine."

Bella was having trouble concentrating. She was vaguely aware of Draken paying the woman. The parade of animals was back in her head, footsteps drumming loudly in her ears. She no longer wanted water—she just wanted to lie down. Yet her legs were rooted, and she was certain they would give out if she tried to take even one step.

Suddenly there was an arm around her shoulders. "Let's get you back."

Bella nodded dumbly as he led her back to the room. She couldn't help but think of Aryia—she desperately wanted her niece back. When she sat down on the bed, tears flooded to her eyes. Embarrassed, she swiped them away, determined not to wallow. Draken knelt in front of her, his face close to hers as he studied her.

"What do you need?" he asked, searchingly.

She gurgled out a laugh. "How did everything get so…wrong?"

Draken stayed quiet, waiting for her new bout of tears to end. She could tell he was uncomfortable. With a sigh, he took her hands, his head bowed forward. Sniffling, Bella felt the tears run freely down her face, but they were no longer so bitter.

When he turned his attention back to her, she could see the determined set of his jaw. "Aleron is safely at Sol. He was injured, but it was minor. I have no news of Azel—only that he searches for her. He is consumed by it. His only thought, besides her, was of you and his children."

They were the most words she'd ever heard Draken speak. Somehow his voice was comforting to her. "And the twins?" Bella asked, relieved to hear that at least her brother was well.

"Safe," Draken replied. He paused, seemed to think better of it, and then added, "I will do everything in my power to find Aryia."

"I know," Bella replied, biting her quivering lip when tears threatened anew. "I feel like it is my fault. I should have been more careful."

He averted his eyes, and shame washed over her. He agreed that she was to blame. Abruptly, he stood and left her. Stunned, she watched him go, unsure what his actions meant. The door closed with a quiet but deafening thud. Panic, pain, and confusion swamped her as she stared down at her limp hands resting lifeless in her lap. Only a moment before they had felt warm and safe in Draken's hands.

Before Bella could recover, Draken entered again, carrying in a dish and a mug. He wet a cloth and held it up to her face. Fresh tears spilled down her cheeks. When she didn't move to take it from him, he hesitantly knelt to wipe at her chin. It stung, but she closed her eyes against the pain. Carefully, he worked across her face as she silently cried for herself and Azel but mostly for Aryia.

Her eyes sprang open when he touched her lip and she jerked away, hissing in pain. His brows furrowed together in concern as she gently reached up to touch her tender lip. Memories of the man who had assaulted her flooded in. Covering her eyes with her hands, she tried to force them away, burying them in black.

She heard Draken sigh, so she peeked through her fingers. His head was bowed, his longer hair having slipped to one side and a few strands hanging in front of his face. Despite the memories, she felt safe. His hand was on the bed beside her, and she instinctively dropped her hand to his. His head came up.

She slipped off the bed. He leaned back as she knelt on the floor with him and wrapped her arms around his broad waist. When she sniffled, his scent rooted in her mind, filling her with a sense of calm and security she hadn't felt since they'd left Sol. Her face was pressed up against his chest.

“This,” Bella whispered, eyes closed. “I need this.”

Suddenly his arms went around her, holding her against him. His hair brushed against her cheek, and his nose was a breath from the top of her head. With a contented sigh, she closed her eyes and melted against him. Her raging headache subsided slightly as she rested against him. He’d always had this effect on her—making her feel protected. His arms were like comforting iron bands and his girth a shield against misery. The only other man besides her brother Aleron who had made her feel safe was Bandon. The same warmth of love existed here—between them in this strange place. Bella’s eyes popped open at the realization that she cared so deeply for Draken. It felt like friendship and yet…she remembered that feeling after Zendar had shook and she’d been hurt. She’d been attracted to him in a fundamentally different way.

As though sensing her eyes on him, Draken opened his own. The amber splashes in the dark brown of his eyes seem to come alive. It caused part of her to remember what it was like to be in a man’s arms. What it had been like to be with Bandon. The sweetness. Yet there was nothing sweet about Draken—he was gruff and unyielding. For a moment, she wondered if his kisses would be the same, if he would be the same with her in a more intimate setting. Instantly, her blood was ignited. Confusion settled in. How could she have such salacious thoughts about Draken?

“I’ll protect you,” he said, the words a rumble in his chest.

Her toes curled instinctively as her body reacted on its own. It wanted him to kiss her. She tipped her head back more to give him access to her lips. Something seemed to pass between them, his eyes dangerously dark. Did he want her in that way as well? He could be so tenderly brutal with her. She yearned for what that promised.

“Drake…” she whispered, her focus dropping to his lips.

Unexpectedly, he hoisted her up. Gasping, she barely recovered before he settled her into bed. He tucked her in like a child, with the sheet all the way up to her throat. He mumbled something about exhaustion and being next door as he made a hasty exit. Bewildered and with a feeling of abandonment, Bella sighed and reached over to get the mug she’d left on the side table. After a few sips while she contemplated what had just happened, Bella returned to a fitful sleep.

Chapter 17:
"Rescue"

"You run it down the board," Vyoma explained, showing her again. "Like this."

The slotted washing board made an odd noise as Vyoma passed sheets across it. Bella had borrowed some of her clothing, though it was much too big for her narrow frame, while she washed her own. She held them balled up and soaking wet as she rested the strange washing board against her legs. Her fingers managed fine on the first few passes, but they grew tired quickly. Though Azel always seemed so at home visiting the kitchens and riding with Aleron, Bella had never taken to household tasks other than sewing. The precision she enjoyed about sewing and embroidery, though, wasn't that much help here.

As she worked, her gaze slid over to the door. She hoped Draken would be back soon with news. Every time she so much as thought of Aryia, she was immediately on the verge of tears. So she tried not think, just work. Sewing rips and washing her clothes would only provide a distraction for so long. Normally she would spend this time with her niece and nephew. She wrung the clothing out, forcing down that train of thought.

"There are drying racks in the room," Vyoma told her with a nod.

As she set the clothing on the wooden brackets in her room, the door opened. She abandoned it and hurried to see who it was. A young boy peeked in as Vyoma stood at the door, wiping her hands on her apron. His hair was short and curly, the darkest black against his deeply tanned skin. He was descended from the Sand People. Of that, Bella was sure.

"What do you want?" Vyoma asked, her face hard.

"I search for the big man," he said, eyes narrow and guarded for someone so young. "I have location he sought. Where he at?" His accent was thick and unfamiliar.

"Aryia," Bella whispered under her breath.

"He's at the Serpent's Tavern," Vyoma said, her manner closed and distrustful.

"I went there first." The boy crossed his arms. "Tell him I came and he miss out."

"Wait!" Bella called, moving swiftly toward him. "I'll go with you."

He scanned her, disbelief in his entire stance. "The Havid are not to be trifled with, lady. Not even sure the big man could handle." The way he said *lady* left much to be desired—as though he thought it an insult.

Vyoma was suddenly next to her. "The Havid?" She turned to Bella. "What did you want with them?"

Bella felt out of her depth. "They have something…of mine." She didn't think it was best to go into details. She addressed the boy. "I'll help you find Draken."

His eyes narrowed. "I don't have all day, lady."

Bella put her hands on her hips, taking the stance she often did with her two nephews when they were unruly. "I'm guessing you want to get paid for your trouble."

The boy glanced at Vyoma, but she said nothing. "Ya." He tried to play off his desire for the coin, but Bella could see he wanted it badly. Part of her heart went out to him. It was in both their interests to find Draken.

"Then let's go." With more confidence then she felt, Bella waved to Vyoma and walked out the door. Her simple shoes tapped on the cobblestone pathway leading to the lazy street in this older district of Ditton.

When they reached the first intersection, she glanced both ways, unsure of where to go next.

"You not from here, are ya?" At least he'd stopped calling her lady.

"No," Bella replied, losing much of her nerve.

"Bella?" Draken's voice startled her from her thoughts. "What are you doing?"

Relief flooded through her. "This boy knows where Aryia is." She gestured at the youngster. "We were coming for you."

He nodded. "I'll take it from here. Go back."

"No." The word was out of Bella's mouth before she knew what she was doing. "I'm coming with you."

His expression of disbelief was quickly replaced with one of sternness. Bella braced herself. "Absolutely not. Go back. Now." Apparently they were back to abrupt responses.

"You'll need my help," Bella insisted, moving closer to make her point. "I'll stay back at a safe distance, but you are but one man." He didn't like it, but she could tell she was wearing him down so she added, "Plus I can defend myself."

The boy laughed, which drew a scowl from both of them. He averted his eyes under their scrutiny before they faced off again. Bella crossed her arms. She wasn't going to take no for an answer. She had failed Aryia before, and she didn't want to do so a second time. This time, she'd be there for her.

"You'll listen to every order I give." It wasn't a question.

"Yes," Bella agreed.

He gave her a curt nod before turning to the boy. "Lead on."

<>

"She's there," the boy said, pointing to a building. "Payment." He held out his hand.

Draken covered the boy's head with one hand. "Partial payment now." He extracted a few coins before depositing them into the boy's open hand. "The rest when I have confirmation."

The boy didn't seem happy about that. "What if you don't make it back?" he grumbled.

Draken gave him a self-assured smirk, and the boy sat down on a massive chunk of rubble, arms crossed, to wait for the rest of his coin.

Frowning, Bella glanced at the destruction around them. This part of the city had been partially destroyed during one of the Bloodline Wars and had never been put right. Apparently, lots of unsavory individuals now called it home. There was something about it that reminded her of the crashed air ship. Perhaps it was because she was afraid and the last time she'd been this afraid had been that moment—the event that started it all.

"Bella." His tone was warning, and it immediately drew her attention.

"Yes?"

He hung his head a moment. "Did you hear what I said?"

The tips of Bella's ears burned. She'd been lost in thought right when she'd needed to prove herself to Draken. Fighting the urge to cry, Bella shifted closer to him, forcing herself to pay attention.

"No, say it again."

He sighed heavily. "There are two men watching the perimeter. I need you to create a distraction so I can get inside to find Aryia." He pointed at the top of the building where two men were.

"What kind of distraction?" Bella asked.

"Something that isn't too obvious," Draken explained. "I'm going to the opening gate. When I'm just outside the gate, cause a distraction. On the opposite side." He gestured in their general direction. "I need you to draw them away. After that, no matter what happens, you need to hide."

The partially broken gate lay precariously half buried in the sand but remained attached by one lower bracket. The rest of the massive stone gate was braced on the back side with stacked boulders, no doubt to keep larger weapons out and prevent a siege.

"Very well," Bella managed, trying to figure out what to do. Sure, she could summon her powers when she needed them most, but only when things were perilous.

His hand was suddenly on her shoulder, and she instinctively met his gaze. "You can do this. This is how we'll save Aryia."

Bella expected to fold under the pressure of what he was asking, but instead she found her ability humming within her chest. It was as determined as she was to help her niece. With a smile, she bent over and picked up a fist-sized stone.

"I'll be ready." Her hand gripped the rubble.

Draken nodded once and then vanished around a wall. Despite her bravado, she was terrified she'd ruin it—that she'd be unable to perform at this critical juncture. Her eyes fell on the boy. A plan began to formulate in her mind. When the boy caught her staring, she waved him over.

"Me?" he whispered.

She nodded and gestured him over with her free hand. "Yes. Come here."

His movements were as hesitant as his face. "What?" he asked, his voice suggesting that he didn't appreciate being asked for anything.

"You look much stronger than me." Bella remembered how much her cousins loved being complimented for their strength—especially LeRoy. "I need you to throw this."

To her surprise, his chest puffed out instantly. "That's easy." He took the stone from her and reeled back.

She immediately waved her hands back and forth. "Not yet."

He froze, mid-wind-up. Easing his frame, he frowned at her. "You should have led with that."

"I'll tell you when." She gave him what she hoped was a winning smile. "You'll be throwing it straight in the air."

His face scrunched up. "What good will that do?"

"I'll take care of the rest." She hoped she would anyway.

Soon, Draken was in position. He carefully peeked at her before vanishing. Bella took a deep breath and called upon her Bloodline. The dirt whooshed around by her feet as she built her ability into a frenzy.

"What's happening?" the boy whispered, his eyes wide in fear.

Bella fought for control as she said through gritted teeth, "Throw it."

He gulped, but the rock left his hand a moment later. It went up at a slight angle, and Bella brought her arms around in a big arc. The wind she created struck the back of the chunk of rubble as it began to come back down. When it connected, the piece hurdled through the air and crashed into the side of the building, immediately drawing everyone's attention that way.

Gasping, Bella dropped behind a boulder with the boy next to her. Their eyes met, and the boy's face spread into a cocky grin. Bella couldn't help but to smile despite the situation. A movement out of the corner of her eye caught her attention. Cautiously, she shifted to see Draken stalking across the open expanse. He moved deftly, his footsteps fast and light. He reminded her of a sandcat.

He vanished around the side of the building. Bella kept herself hidden as she slid around to try and spot him. He hadn't gone through the front doors like she would have thought. Her eyes scanned the building, hunting for movement that wasn't the guards. As one of the guards on the rooftop walked by, Draken appeared and yanked him over the side. Bella's heart was beating wildly in suspense as the first guard disappeared from view and the second guard turned around.

The other guard called out, drew his sword, and went to the roof's edge. Bella couldn't make out what he was saying. When the guard went towards the front and called over the side to his compatriots, Draken crept onto the roof before locking him in a headlock. He struggled, trying to stab his sword back and into Draken, but Draken easily disarmed him, his bulky arm still locked around his throat. Eventually the guard stopped struggling.

Without hesitation, Draken disappeared off the roof by going over the backside. Lightheaded, Bella exhaled. She hadn't realized she'd been holding her breath. After a moment, Draken reappeared, creeping around the side as another man appeared from the lone building. The new man called up to the now incapacitated guard as the door swung closed behind him. Shifting, he spotted Draken. Bella's hands clenched into fists in apprehension. A second later, Draken punched the man in the throat. He stumbled back, clutching his neck.

Draken's fist collided with his head a moment later, sending him crashing against the wall. As Draken stepped over the man's prone form, two other men burst out of the same door, swords in hand. Draken blocked the first attack with ease and delivered a punch that sent him reeling back. Back and forth they went, Draken wearing them down. When three more men appeared, Bella's stomach jumped to her throat.

One man fell and then another. Another man cut across Draken's arm. Bella gasped, but then realized how small the injury was, how little blood it had brought forth.

The boy tugged at her arm. "Get down," he cautioned. She hadn't realized that she'd gotten to her feet, no longer hidden completely behind the boulder.

A large man pushed his way through the door holding two long slender pieces of metal in each hand. Five against one was one thing, but this giant was even bigger than Draken. She yanked free of the boy's grasp and was up and over the boulder before she knew was she was doing. Her wind on her back, she half-floated and half-sprinted down the rubble, her powers growing into a hot knot at her core.

Draken cut another of the smaller men down, but doing so left him exposed on one side. The big man's thin weapon caught him on the ribs. Draken faltered, parried a blow from another man, and staggered back. Before the big man could attack again, Bella let loose the ferocity of her ability. It slammed into the giant and sideswiped two others into the building's wall.

The smaller two were crumbled and dazed, but the giant was still standing. He had lost one of the weapons, but he held the other tight in his hand as he advanced on Bella. It was only then that she realized what she'd done. Fear twisted in her gut as she stumbled back, trying to call up another powerful attack against the angry man who stalked toward her.

She backed into a pile of rubble, and her legs buckled. She went over backward and landed hard between two chunks. As Bella scrambled to get up, the giant lifted his weapon with murder in his eyes.

The tip of a sword blossomed in his chest. His face was wide with surprise as he opened his mouth. Blood gurgled out as the metal piece fell to the ground, glancing off the stone to her left. As he fell to his knees, the ground shook beneath her. Behind him, Draken yanked his sword back, causing the man to slump to the side, struggling for breath.

"I told you to stay," Draken said, a dark expression on his face.

"I know," Bella said, shaking uncontrollably.

His expression softened, and he offered her a hand. She took it hesitantly, and he helped her to her feet. Once standing, she saw the bodies lying across the yard. Most were unmoving. Were they were dead? It had been some time since Bella had seen death. She had to remind herself these were men, though, who had taken Aryia and had perhaps hurt her.

The thought of Aryia spurred her into action. Draken caught her arm before she could take more than two steps. "Where are you going?"

"To get Aryia," Bella replied, her mind foggy, dazed.

He sighed and hung his head a moment before turning back to the building. "I don't know how many more there are. It isn't safe."

She glanced at the two men who were still motionless where she'd flung them. "They can't have more than one giant." Though she'd meant the words seriously, his face broke into an amused smirk.

He nodded. "Stay behind me."

Turning, he held his sword at the ready as he stalked toward the building. They were nearly there when a man came out with his hand on Aryia's shoulder and a short dagger to her throat. Her hair was tousled and her dress smeared with dust and grim. Despite looking tired, though, she appeared unharmed.

"Make her give it back," the man yelled, the blade poised for damage. Aryia didn't appear worried. It wasn't anger in his voice, it sounded more like…desperation?

She took in the streaks of sweat on his brow and the tears of despair, and in an instant Bella knew what Aryia had done. Draken gripped the hilt of his blade.

"Put down the blade," Bella heard herself say. "And I'll tell her to fix you."

A sob gurgled up his throat as he dropped the weapon. Aryia didn't seem to be all there, her eyes indifferent as the man collapsed beside her, begging to have "it" back. Clearly, she'd taken whatever Bloodline he'd been gifted with.

"Aryia." Bella moved cautiously forward. "You can give it back."

"He doesn't deserve Zendar's gift," Aryia whispered. "He is a bad man." The detachment in her voice terrified Bella to her core.

The man gripped the bottom of Aryia's tattered dress. "Please!" He was sobbing now. "I won't survive. I must have it. Give it back."

Bella took a step forward, moving past Draken, who was tense but still, no doubt confused by what was happening. "I know." Bella tried to keep her voice calm, like she was talking to a frightened animal. "I know he scared you, probably hurt you. But does Zendar wish this?"

Aryia seemed to consider her words. After a moment, she touched the man's head. He collapsed at her feet, thanking her, and Aryia seemed to snap out of it. She locked her eyes on Bella and bolted straight into her arms. Bella held her niece close as she cried. Draken gave Bella a questioning look, but she shook her head. Now was not the time—plus she didn't know what to tell him.

Chapter 18:
"Walker to Runner"

After they returned and she'd washed, Aryia went straight to sleep. Bella stared at her sleeping face, her hand moving in circular motions on the girl's back until her breathing evened out. Tomorrow would be another day, a day to face what Aryia had gone through, but sleep was a great healer. Bella's hand went instinctively her to side as the memories of the assassin swirled in her mind. Sleep and time healed most everything.

Gathering up her clothing, Bella went to bathe. When she reached the two doors, she saw that the one on the right was cracked slightly. She could see Draken's bulk. He was bent over the sink, his shirt removed as he inspected the bruise on his side. She gasped when she saw it spreading purple, red, and blue.

"It's worse than it looks." He turned away.

She pushed the door open. "Let me see."

He moved away from her like she was diseased. "You shouldn't be in here."

There was red on his temple. "You're bleeding." She went to the sink and picked up a rag. "Let me help."

Draken didn't seem like he was going to reply, so she fixed him with her best indignant stare. After a moment, he dropped down onto the tub's stone side. The bathing area was taller than she was used to seeing—a remnant of old times when they'd had more water. Carefully, she wiped the blood on his face and then went to work on cleaning the nasty cut.

"What a pair we make." Bella hadn't even seen her own bruises and cuts yet. She'd been too afraid to find a mirror.

He chuckled. "Your brother will not think so."

Bella paused and focused on his features. The hard edges of his face, his too-big nose, and his very thick neck did not lend him looks that she could call attractive. Even the beard only made him look gruff. Despite that, there was something around his eyes and the way his mouth seemed to take on a specific expression whenever she was near.

Bella had no idea what it meant, but she liked it. Butterflies danced in her stomach as she felt heat lace through her veins, her mind wondering what that mouth would taste like.

"Is it clean?" His gravelly voice was pitched low.

"Hmm?" Bella asked, lost in thoughts. Slowly, she blinked them from her vision. "What did you say?"

He turned to her, his eyes impossibly dark brown and filled with something akin to desire. "Are you done?" He carefully took the cloth from her.

"Oh. Oh!" She blinked. "Yes." Her ears burning, she scurried out of the room and into the other bathing area. She closed the door and leaned against it, her mind reeling. What in the world had she been thinking?

<>

Moonlight cast a shadow through the narrow slits in the wall. Bella tossed and turned on the bed, Aryia sleeping next to her. Sitting up, she saw the massive orb of the Runner, knowing his little brother, Walker, was just behind him. The two moons of Zendar. Suddenly, Bella realized she was the Walker. She never ran after what she wanted, just let everything happen. A surge of courage laced through her body as she cracked open the door to her room. Slipping along the wall, she went to Draken's room. Her hand hovered on the handle, and she nearly turned back when she heard his bed creak.

She clasped the handle and slipped into the room. Moonlight cast three slits of light across the room. Draken's large shape was situated on the bed, his back to her. When the door settled into place behind her, he sat up, cold steel in his hand, the moonlight glinting off it with menacing promise.

"Drake?" Bella whispered, creeping further into the room.

His posture relaxed. "Is something wrong?"

Bella shrugged, her face burning at her plans. "I couldn't sleep." She boldly strode over to him as he stood up.

He towered over her, but instead of feeling intimidated, she felt a deep-seated desire take root—it emboldened her. She went onto her tiptoes and wrapped her arms around his neck. He pulled back in confusion but then held still. His face was etched with concerned.

"Bella?" His hot breath was on her face, smelling of sweet wine.

As an answer, she kissed him. The moment their lips touched, she felt a jolt to her core. It was subdued, though, because he wasn't returning her kiss. She shifted back and his eyes were wide open in shock.

"What are you doing?" he demanded, his voice surprisingly husky.

Bella bit her lip in nervousness but didn't let go. "Kiss me?"

He took hold of her waist and tried to push her down. "You are a girl. Confused by recent events. I am old enough to be your father."

Instead of relenting, anger boiled up within her. She tightened her hold so they were face to face. "But you aren't my father. I know exactly what I want!"

She drove forward to kiss him again, her lips brushing against his before he pulled his head back. "Bella stop it." He pried her off with ease, despite her protest.

Her powers rose up within her, and she shoved him back. He stumbled until he was against the wall. Bella wasted no time in throwing herself back around his neck and kissed him again, this time in earnest. She was unbridled, the surge of freedom hot in her veins as all pretense and fear fell away.

To her surprise, he kissed her back. Her knees felt weak at the feel of his facial hair against her face. The rough forcefulness of his lips made her forget what she was doing and allowed her to only *be*. The wave of sticky sweetness wrapped itself around her, drowning her in promises of what else he could show her.

When she tried to deepen the kiss, leaning into him, she felt him restrain himself. "Is that all?" Bella asked, breathing heavily but far from sated. "Don't hold back."

With a gasp of surprise, he dumped her on the bed. She bounced slightly as he growled, "You don't know what fire you are playing with." The junction between her legs vibrated with anticipation.

Instead of showing her, though, Draken began walking around the bed, and Bella realized he intended to leave. She snatched up a pillow and threw it at him. It bounced off his shoulder harmlessly.

She stood. "I'm not done with you."

"This cannot continue," Draken told her, his entire face dark.

Adrenaline and recklessness twisted in her belly. Instead of answering, she jumped on him like a feral cat, latching onto him. He whirled around and pinned her against the wall. "You are a child. You do not know what you are asking."

Bella heard his words but didn't believe him. She could feel his arousal against her side. Its bulge belayed what his body wanted of her, even if his mind didn't agree. He had her arms pinned, so she went to her tiptoes and pressed her hips against him.

"If I were a child, could I stir such desire?" Bella asked confidently as she strained against his hold.

His expression looked almost pained as he closed his eyes. She tipped her head to the side as she moved forward to kiss him again to break his resolve. Nothing else mattered in this moment but him and what he was doing to her. He made her feel alive. What other wonderful things he could do to her?

"Drake, I want—" she began, but he abruptly pushed away from her.

"You are a fool." Each word echoed in her head as time slowed, the look of disgust on his face clear.

Bella swallowed hard, tears forming in her eyes. Shame over her wonton behavior paralyzed her. What had been freeing only moments before wound itself around her and tightened until she could barely breathe. He left the room and she sunk back against the wall, sliding down it. She curled into a ball on the floor, crying into her knees as she hugged them against her chest. She had been sure she'd seen something in his eyes, admiration or even affection. Once she'd even thought she'd seen lust, which had given her the courage to try to push past her reservations and the pain Bandon's death still brought her sometimes late at night. And what had she gotten for it? Rejection.

<>

Draken wanted to punch something. Bella had him so worked up that he was spoiling for a fight. He stomped from the room, his fists flexing in anger and frustration. What could she be thinking? There was absolutely no way she felt that for him.

He was disgusted with himself that he *did* want her. She was alone and scared—he could not allow his mind to be ruled by his body. It would be taking advantage of her. Plain and simple, he was the closest person she could latch onto. She'd just grasped at anything to help with the fear, even pleasure with someone much older than her.

He paused in the middle of the street. That wasn't Bella. She could be impulsive and sometimes indecisive, but she wasn't a whore. He ran a hand over his face before scratching the back of his head. He couldn't betray Aleron. His Liege had trusted him to bring Bella home safely. He'd trusted Draken with his beloved sister.

He couldn't be what she wanted of him. Turning, he went back into the building and toward his room to tell her that. The need to be honest was overwhelming. She'd always been special to him, but there was so much Bella didn't know about him. There were so many things he couldn't share with her.

Chapter 19:
"Love has Many Faces"

Bella was still crying on the floor when she felt a hand on her shoulder. Lifting her head in surprise, she saw Draken's concerned face. Sniffling, she waited for him to say something. Instead he hesitated.

"What?" Bella asked, embarrassed at how pathetic her voice sounded.

"I'm sorry," Draken said, and Bella instinctively shrunk away from him and his pity.

Taking a steadying breath, she realized that if he didn't want her when she was throwing herself at him, he never would. Instead of crying about it, she needed to let him go, let any dream she had and all the feelings she had wither and die. They would always be there, but she needed to move on from the hope that there could be something more.

His expression of concern was almost painful, and she hated that she was responsible for it. She wanted him to be happy. "I understand." Bella patted his hand. "I'm not desirable. I'm sorry that I tried to force my wishes on you. That wasn't fair." Despite her resolve, the wound of his rejection was too fresh and her eyes burned from the rush of emotion. "I'm not what you want." The words were choked out as she turned her face away to hide her tears.

"You are beautiful." She turned back to him in surprise. "It is you who doesn't know me, know what I've done. Aleron may have become the Liege that brought peace, but that was only because of Azel. He changed because of her. I am what I am, and not even you and your innocence can change that." He leaned forward and kissed her gently, a kiss that made her heart ache. "I cannot give you what you want. I don't want a family, or a wife. I can be nothing more. Aleron trusted me to bring you home to him safely. No matter how determined you are, I cannot be with you."

Bella tried to absorb his words but failed. She considered what he was telling her. It wasn't that he didn't desire her; it was that he couldn't offer her what Bandon and she'd had. Did she even want that? To her surprise, the answer was no. She just wanted to find out what that zing behind his kisses was.

Her bruised heart mended slightly at the thought. "I've been a wife. I do not want that. I loved my husband, but he didn't stir this need that you do. When you kissed me, I couldn't think. I believe that is desire."

Surprised crossed his face. "I'm no good for you," he said, but she could tell his major objection was no longer an issue. "Sometimes love and lust are hard to separate." Draken shook his head. "It is too great of a risk."

"I already love you," Bella said, and laughed at the shocked expression on his face. "You've always been a friend to me. A good one. I trust you, but I don't love you like I did Bandon." Bella could remember the intimacy with Bandon and how much he'd meant to her. He'd been her heart. That wasn't how she felt about Draken. "Bandon's body struggled…" Bella's face burned at the admission.

He moved his hand up to her shoulder. "I understand."

Bella shifted toward him. "Will you show me what passion is?" She froze in surprise when he nodded.

"On my terms."

Afraid to speak, sure that he would retract his acceptance, Bella silently bobbed her head in consent. Carefully, as if approaching a terrified animal, Draken touched her cheek, his rough fingers sending waves of heat down her neck, through her chest, and pooling between her legs. Bringing his face closer, he opened his mouth and kissed her like he was going to consume her. Her brain emptied as she clung to him, certain that if she let go she would be reduced to a pile of mush. His facial hair added an extra zing to his kiss.

Effortlessly, he lifted her up without breaking the kiss. She felt weightless in his arms as he set her on the bed. Her fingers sought out flesh while he plundered her mouth, his tongue making her toes curl. She started to pull at the buckles that held his leather armor on, frustrated but unwilling to break the connection of their lips.

Chuckling, he eased back. "I'll do it." His husky voice sent shivers of pleasure through her body.

A few deft movements, and the armor was up over his head. He was built like a bull, with a firm torso that matched his rippling arms.

He had black hair across his chest and a second patch of hair that ran down his stomach and disappeared into his pants. She'd never seen so much hair on a man's chest!

When he leaned forward, Bella thought he was going to kiss her again, but instead he nuzzled her neck and slid his tongue across the bottom of her ear. His beard tickled her neck, but it only made her want more. She jolted at the sensitivity, pressing her hands against his chest. He moved down her neck, nipping and licking wherever he liked. The world fell away until all that remained was the feeling of his touch and her own mounting pleasure.

His hands cupped her left breast, his dark eyes watching her as he teased the nipple through the fabric. The layer of separation did little to dull her sensitivity. She arched when he clamped onto her nipple with his mouth. His teeth applied just the right amount of pressure to leave her gasping.

"Drake," she cried out instinctively.

He chuckled against her breast. "You'll want to keep quiet. I'm not sure the owner would be happy about this."

Bella swallowed as she nodded her head, not sure how she was going to keep herself in check. He made her irrational, and it was wonderful. She'd never felt so free before—the passion was liberating. Another assault on her nipple caused her to clap a hand over her mouth to keep the bubbling exclamation in check. Her mind was split between the growing need and the narrow focus on keeping her responses muted.

He worked his way down her stomach as Bella glanced down at the top of his head. She knew what he intended to do, and Bella squeezed her eyes closed to block out the rising embarrassment. It felt foolish after her earlier behavior, but no one but her husband had seen that intimate part of her before. Was it normal? Bandon hadn't complained or said anything, but he'd been as innocent as her. Bella doubted Draken was celibate.

Something brushed against her cheek, and Bella's eyes flew open. Draken's face was hovering close to hers, her fingers brushing against her skin. "Relax," he said, his voice gruff but filled with warmth. "You're beautiful."

That was all it took. The gentle look in his eye and three words caused all the tension and fear to rush out of her. Instinctively, she reached for him, her arms wrapping around his thick neck as she crushed her lips to his. His hands roamed over her body, moving down, but Bella focused on his mouth. Plundering it. Tasting him.

When his fingers pushed up her robe, Bella found only anticipation. Her underclothing was in the next room, still drying after their washing, so there was nothing between his fingers and her. His finger swept across her opening, touching the sensitive nerve endings, and Bella's toes curled as her back arched. His touch was like lightening.

She began to squirm with pleasure as his fingers began to explore her inner folds. All thought deserted her as she broke off their kiss, unable to concentrate. She clung to him and then pushed away from him, fighting down the rising need to exclaim her delight at what he was doing to her. Relentlessly, he drove her up and up, his fingers working in and out of her. Little moans escaped her. She felt him shift away from her, and for a moment she protested until his tongue joined his fingers.

Whatever had been holding her back shattered, and she felt a sudden rush flood her body. She gasped, her eyes wide, her body arching on the bed. Her legs locked around his shoulders. When the energy started to subside Bella found herself breathless, a sense of euphoria settling in.

"Oh," Bella finally managed, glancing down at Draken. "Oh my."

When their eyes locked, Bella started giggling. She couldn't help it. Draken seemed taken aback until she reached for him, and then he chuckled. Sliding up the length of her, he settled directly beside her, his heat radiating into her. Bella couldn't stop laughing, chuckles racking her body as the giddy feeling subsided.

When she finally was able to control herself, she touched the side of his face. "Thank you."

He leaned forward and kissed the top of her forehead. "You will love again." The words were hardly a whisper.

Overwhelmed, Bella felt tears prick her eyes. She buried her face against his chest, ignoring the tickle of his chest hair. He put a massive arm around her, drawing her against him. Despite what had happened, there was this comfortable comradery between them. It brought her immense relief that that hadn't changed.

Breathing in his manly scent reminded her that Draken hadn't completely participated. Bella's mind immediately wandered to what it would feel like to have him inside of her. Her face burned at the thought that he must be as big everywhere.

Unable to look him in the eye because of how embarrassed she was, Bella practically whispered, "I'm ready."

He grunted. "What?"

Draken moved back so her words weren't muffled against his chest. Bella felt her safety net fall away. Instead of shying away, she lifted her face and repeated her offering. He appeared confused at first and then his face relaxed.

"I'm tired," he replied. "Maybe tomorrow."

He drew her back against him as his heavy arm draped lazily across her shoulder. The bulge against her leg felt anything but tired. Unwilling to protest and push her luck, remembering this was on his terms, Bella snuggled up against him and let sleep slowly take hold. After an exciting day and an equally eventful evening, it took little effort.

<>

Somehow Draken's not getting pleasure justified for him his actions. He had fully intended to do nothing to her, had fully intended to comfort and return her to her room. Then she'd smashed all expectations, taken all his arguments and shattered them. She loved him, but not that way. She only wanted to know pleasure since her husband had been unable to. She'd wanted him to show her.

Draken hadn't even known he was going to agree until the words were out of his mouth. He wished he could blame his other brain for taking over, but he knew that was the choice both heads would have come to in the end. Denying Bella what she wanted had never been one of Draken's strong suits. Sure he'd picked on her and protected her, but at the end of the day, he would have lain down his life for hers—at first out of duty, but later out of an unconventional friendship.

He'd expected that line they'd just crossed, the line he was imagining still existed, would change that. Instead, that same comfortableness remained. Despite that, though, the taste of her, the memory of her surprised mewing and little gasps—and the way she uttered his name, the name only she called him—all of it made his manhood harder until it was almost unbearable. He'd thought it would quickly subside, but now her sweet scent and little body was pressed up against him.

And while it was one thing for her to trust him, it was another level of trust altogether to fall sleep almost instantly while he was still hard against her. Even now, as he leaned back and inspected her sleeping face, completely trusting that he would protect her, he wanted to drive her back to that brink of pleasure. If he wasn't careful, she'd become an addiction. Realizing he needed to take action, he slowly slipped out of her hold, covered her with a thin blanket, and hurried off to handle his growing need himself before all reason left him.

Chapter 20:
"Change in Perspective"

Bella was smitten. As she walked beside Draken with Aryia's hand in hers, she studied his face. Had he always been so adorable? Something about his gruff exterior made her want to smother him with kisses. She resisted the urge—barely. He glanced at her, his brows pressed down in a scowl. It just broadened her smile further. Wherever they ended up tonight, she fully intended to return the favor for last night. Confidence and determination surged through her.

As they reached the medium-sized air ship, Bella wondered how many days she'd have left with him. Her heart sank. Once they returned, this part of their relationship would end.

Aryia's hand tightened around hers. "What's wrong?" Aryia whispered.

Bella smiled at her dear niece. "Nothing. Just not excited to be in one of these again so quickly."

Draken opened the back and gestured for them to go in. "Come on. Don't dawdle."

Normally Bella would have prickled at his gruffness, perhaps even retorted, but now he was just… adorable. What an odd word to uses to describe Draken. Aryia went first with Draken helping her aboard.

"Will we make it home today?" Bella asked, carefully keeping as much emotion out of her voice as possible as she strapped into one of the two passenger seats. This ship was bigger than the one Bella had piloted.

"No," Draken replied, clicking buttons as he settled into the pilot's seat. "We'll have to stop and camp for one night."

Bella turned her eyes downcast as she halfheartedly checked her straps. "I thank you."

They were waved from their spot and then shot out down the ramp that led to the sands. Bella swallowed instinctively, remembering how close they'd come to perishing in the dunes. If it weren't for Aryia, they surely would have been inside a sand viper's gullet right now, being digested. Bella reached out and gripped her hand. Aryia's eyes were full of unconditional love as they held tight. This adventure would bond them together—forever. In time, Aryia's hand slipped from her fingers as the girl craned her neck at a passing rock formation.

After riding in silence for a while, Bella remembered she'd had little to no sleep the night before. Her cheeks burned at the memory of why, and she settled in for a long ride. Focusing on what she could see of him, Bella daydreamed about what it would be like to be with him inside of her. The salacious thoughts made her blush extend to her ears.

Adjusting the way she was sitting, Bella rested her head back and closed her eyes. It wasn't long before the gentle hum of the ship and the warmth of the day lulled her into a peaceful sleep.

<>

Something tugging at her arm woke her up. Bella yawned as she glanced over at Aryia's excited face. "Time for lunch."

Chuckling, Bella unbuckled her seat and rose. Still having to duck slightly, she went over to the storage cabinets in the floor from which she extracted some fruit, cheese, and bread. As she tore pieces off, she glanced in Draken's direction. He continued to pilot the ship with unwavering dedication. As irrational as it was, she wanted his attention. Their time was short together, and once they returned, the affable-but-not-sexual relationship would resume. Drake would return to his place, and she would return to hers.

Despite her having told him she understood this, it was still disheartening. They had only just begun—whatever it was they were doing—and yet it was coming to an end. Part of her had been worried the morning after would be filled with regret or awkwardness, but instead their friendship had endured. He was driven by duty, so Bella knew he wouldn't ever approach her. It would be up to Bella to decide the next move.

Food prepared and divided, she handed the cloth to Aryia. Her niece had been rattling off what she knew about the ruins they were going to. Bella had been too absorbed in her own thoughts but knew it was something about a princess who had been stolen for a bride by their ancestor. As she talked about it, Bella realized how much her world had changed. What had once been common practice, even when she was child, had ended in Aryia's lifetime. Arranged marriages were still commonplace, but stolen brides were a rare occurrence and staunchly discouraged. In a way it had ended with Azel—the last stolen bride.

She brought the food to Draken, who engaged the primary controls before taking the sandwich. He spared her a glance and a word of gratitude but little else. Disappointed, she returned to her own food, eating slowly and deliberately as she contemplated what to do next. Determined not to be impacted by his apparent indifference, Bella turned her entire attention to Aryia. They played games, spoke of times past, and even reminisced about their adventure.

Hours passed before Draken told them to strap in. Aryia pointed out the ruins, and Bella strained in her seat to see around Draken's girth. When they swept to the right, their destination came into full view. Simple stone with no roof but high walls. Draken easily navigated the ship into a perfect landing pad. She'd wondered if other people would be there, but they were alone.

Bella took in the smooth, weathered stone. The walls rose above her to towering heights, and to their left was a wide opening. When Bella stood to leave the ship, Draken stopped her. Aryia clung to her side as Draken opened the back hatch.

"Let me secure the area." He was gone before she could respond, swiftly moving around the ship.

Her mind wandered to the battle and his Kaheron Bloodline. Like her brother, Draken was immensely powerful, his body built to deliver damage. The thought of what he could do with that strength sent shivers down her spine. She was turning into a depraved daydreamer!

She tried to focus instead on the ruined structure where they would be making camp. It was about the size of their banquet area in Sol. When she leaned to see more inside, she could discern a few more walls and even a makeshift sitting area with fallen stone blocks.

When he reappeared she asked, "Everything clear?"

"Yes." He slung one bag over his arm and then another. "Let's make camp."

Chapter 21:
"A Rough Childhood"

Bella tucked Aryia in and kissed her forehead. "We're almost there."

Aryia's eyes drooping in exhaustion as she gathered the blanket on her cot under her chin. She nodded at Bella's words, and muttered "Good night" before drifting off. Bella loved her all the more for it. As she crawled into her own cot, the lamp light fading, she felt restless. Her mind wouldn't quiet as she struggled with the knowledge this was her and Draken's last night together.

After a moment, she slipped from the bed and out into the opening. A fire crackled, and Draken was watching the door. He lifted his head as she approached. Suddenly shy under his gaze, she sat down to his left. Staring into the flames, she struggled to find the right words.

"You know this cannot continue," Draken told her, his voice hushed.

She slid across the makeshift stone bench toward him. "Once was not enough."

He grunted. "It will have to be."

Bella pouted, unhappy with what was happening. "I don't accept that."

His eyebrows rose. "My terms, remember?"

"I remember," she grumbled. "You also agreed to show me pleasure. I cannot imagine last night was it."

A grin tugged at his lips before he was able to stifle it. He replaced it with a scowl, but she had seen the truth. "That is a line I am unwilling to cross. Go back to bed, Bella. Tomorrow you'll be home with your brother."

Bella saw right through him. He was putting Aleron between them. She rocketed to her feet, startling him as she reached out a hand. "Then we won't cross it."

He stared at her outstretched hand as though it were a sand viper, poised to strike. She waited patiently, knowing he was likely to cave to her request. Finally, he reached out and took her hand, but when she tugged him toward the tent, he jerked back. Caught off guard, she tumbled into his lap.

Gasping, she glanced up at his face, an indigent feeling in her core making her blush. Opening her mouth to censure him, she stopped when she saw his smiling face, which made his dark brown eyes shine. He was teasing her.

Two could play that game! Bella thought as she looped an arm around his neck, lifting herself toward his face. The slight rumble in his chest stopped immediately.

Bella stroked a hand across the sides of his head where his hair had been trimmed close to his sculp. "Why'd you cut your hair?" she asked, purposely pressing herself closer than was necessary to caress his head.

"I wanted something different," Draken replied, his voice pitched low. It made parts of her vibrate with excitement. "This is an ancient warrior's style."

"Hmm." Absentmindedly, she gently raked her nails across his scalp. "I like it." Then she turned to his face and touched his beard. "And the beard is a part of that?"

"Yes." The words were husky, and she knew she was having an effect on him.

Her fingers traced from his cheek to his lips. "I've never properly kissed a man with a beard before you."

"What do you think you're doing?" he asked, her hands on her waist, likely trying to hold her in place at a satisfactory distance.

"I won't be able to be this close to you again," Bella replied with a sigh. "I want to enjoy it while I can."

He leaned his head against her forehead, exhaling heavily. "I don't believe you've worn me down."

Using her hands, she lifted his face. "Yes you do." Then she kissed him softly. Wrapping her arms around his neck, she let herself drown in the passion.

When they parted, she kissed his nose. His brows furrowed in confusion, and she slid off his lap and bolted toward his tent. He tried to swipe at her, and instinctively she propelled herself forward with her power. Wind gently made the tent entrance flap and her dress dance; her hair was wild around her face as she turned back.

Draken had stopped chasing her and was just staring. They stayed like that as the wind died down before she slipped into the tent. The moment she did, the heady scent that always seemed to accompany him assaulted her senses. Bella felt lightheaded knowing he'd follow her in a moment toward the lone cot. She sat on it and waited. A minute passed, and then another. Was he really not going to come? She imagined him pacing, likely in turmoil, but Bella trusted him. He wouldn't disappoint her.

Finally, the flap opened and he entered. When his eyes rested on her sitting on his cot, he gave her a lopsided grin. She reached up to fix her hair, sure the wind had ruffled it into complete chaos.

"What's so funny?" Bella demanded, glancing around.

"You're so much smaller than my bed," Draken replied. When her jaw dropped open, he candidly laughed.

"So what if I'm small!" Bella shot to her feet and strode up to him.

Before she could continue her outraged speech, he reached out, grabbed her around the waist, and lifted her. Her eyes were opened wide in shock when he kissed her. With a sigh, she relaxed against him as he held her in the air and plundered her mouth.

Panting, they parted, leaving her with a euphoric feeling similar to having an excess of wine. Her limbs were slow to respond as she admired him. Impossibly, every day he became a little more handsome to her, as though his power and playful attitude infused his very being.

"What exactly did you have in mind?" Draken asked, each word sounding hesitant, as though he was uncertain of the question, or at least of the answer.

Bella barely had to consider his words. She already knew what she wanted. "There is sand on you." She wiped at some on his forehead. "Let me wash you." Washing was an intimate gesture, but she didn't know how else to see and touch all of him.

His eyebrows furrowed. "I don't think that's a good idea." He went to set her down.

"I'll keep my clothes on!" Bella held fast to his neck as he grabbed her upper arms.

"I won't expose myself for your curiosity." His eyes were dark, as though she'd mocked him in some way.

Bella pursed her lips. "Bandon didn't like me touching him. He was very sensitive about my seeing his legs. I want to see you. All of you." Despite the boldness of her words, her cheeks were scalding hot.

His hands were back on her waist, his eyes studying her face. Whatever he was searching for he must have found…or didn't find…because he nodded. This time when he stepped back, reaching down for the buckles on his armor, she let him go. Her eyes searched for the washing bin. It would contain everything they needed.

"It is there." Draken gestured towards a bag. "On the left side."

The bag was heavy as she pried it open. It took a little rummaging, but soon she extracted the telltale sack. When she turned around, he was kneeling, completely nude. Clenching the pouch to her chest, she took in all of him. His thighs budged with muscles, his hands resting on them. His chest was sturdy and angled slightly to his hips. Her eyes lingered on the trail of hair as warm slickness pooled at the junction between her legs. Perhaps Draken had been right—perhaps this was a bad idea. Just seeing him like that, and she wanted to break all his silly rules.

His head was bowed at first, but when she didn't move he glanced up at her. Playfully, he cleared his throat, bringing her back to reality. When she drew closer she saw the fading bruise on his chest. The lamplight cast just enough that she could see it. She carefully poured some water onto a cloth.

Shyly, she began to wipe away the dust, rewetting the cloth as needed. When she saw a prominent scar, her fingers instinctively traced over it. Draken reacted for the first time since she'd started, grunting, as though telling her to move on. Despite the thin line she was walking, Bella traced the next scar she saw and the next.

Wringing out the cloth she asked, "Why do you have so many?"

"I'm your brother's warrior," Draken replied.

Bella traced one on his shoulder. "This one is so faded. You've had some of these for years and years." They reminded Bella of the scar on her abdomen.

Draken's eyes were guarded as Bella carefully continued cleaning his hard planes. "That one is from when I was a boy."

It was more than the monosyllable or withheld response she'd expected. Blinking, she paused in her cleaning to look up at him as she knelt on one knee beside him. He didn't meet her gaze. She'd never thought of Draken as a child, but it was true he had been at one time. She could not imagine him ever being smaller then her, it boggled the mind.

She lifted one of his hands as she cleaned along his arm. He relented, but she could see the tension in his back. When she finished that arm she moved to the other. Humming with questions, she grew antsy, struggling to contain them.

Halfway through his other arm, he let out a loaded sigh. "You're literally vibrating with questions."

Caught and feeling a little ashamed, but mostly embarrassed, she ducked her head. Without thought, her eyes locked directly onto his manhood. When they'd started it had been partially flaccid, but now it had grown considerably in size and rigidity. Seeing that brought on a feeling of triumphant glee that pushed her lack of self-confidence aside.

"You've never talked about your childhood," Bella replied, returning to the task at hand, though her eyes strayed from time to time.

Again a heavy exhale as she returned to twist the old water out. She took out the oils and gathered them in her hands. She planned to finish washing his lower half, the dangerous part, after the first part was done—just in case something *did* happen. She started rubbing oil on his back, her small hands against his thick muscles. Her eyes nearly popped out of her head when his member stiffened the rest of the way. It was massive! Looking up, she focused on the bruise knowing the oils would protect his skin and help with healing. When she peeked at his face, she noticed his eyes had a distant, far-off look to them.

"I lived on the street as a child." The words were barely audible.

Bella paused. "I didn't know that." He shifted uncomfortably, and her heart went out to him. She timidly touched his shoulder. "You don't have to share. I don't want to pry."

"Any more then you already have?" Despite the seriousness of the conversation, his words were good-natured.

Bella thought about it for a moment, amused but not easily persuaded. "Perhaps it is just that you know everything about me, but I know so little about you."

He reached up and enveloped her hand with his. It was the first time he'd touched her since his cleaning had begun. Although she was standing and he was kneeling, his head was just under her chin. She had the sudden urge to kiss him, but she was too determined to find out more about him.

"I was raised in a high-end brothel until I was ten. My mother was a concubine who was killed, and being a boy I was left to fend for myself," he told her, his face stony. "It is a time I do not like to dwell on."

It was everything Bella could do to keep the tears at bay. "You were orphaned young, like I was."

"Yes," he replied, releasing her hand and turning back to his sitting position with his fists on his thighs. "In that we are the same."

She threw her arms around his neck, hugging him tightly from the back and burying her face against his neck. He'd stiffened at first, but she could feel his shoulders relaxing after a few moments. His heady scent filled her nose as it twined with the sweet smell of raspberries and lemon from the oil.

"Your clothes are going to be covered with oil now." The words were a rumble in his chest, and she liked the way it felt.

"I don't care," she whispered against his neck. "I want to make the bad memories go away."

Twisting around, he snagged his arm around her waist and pulled her around to the front of him. She let out a yip of surprise. He held her against him, her arms crushed between them as he nuzzled his face against her hair. Closing her eyes, she leaned into him, accepting the comfort of his embrace.

Shifting, he rested his forehead against hers. "Never change."

Chapter 22:
"Family"

In the morning Bella woke and stretched like the furry pets Azel kept. Despite the fact that nothing sexual had happened and he'd sent her straight to bed, she was satisfied. She'd learned something about him that she felt few people knew. Sighing contently, she turned her head and saw an empty cot beside her. She bolted upright and was out of the cot and through the door in the blink of an eye.

Draken was loading the sacks into the ship. His tent was already collapsed. It took her a moment to spot Aryia. Standing, eyes focused on the horizon, she was embraced in a halo of light. It made her glow, and for a moment Bella was transfixed. When she turned her head, she seemed much older, her wise eyes seeing beyond the world itself.

"Good morning," Draken said, nodding to her. With that, the spell was broken, and Aryia turned back. "You'll want to get dressed."

Blushing when she realized she only wore a thin camisole instead of the oil-covered nighttime clothing Vyoma had sold her, Bella bounded back into the tent. Cheeks burning, she quickly changed before she started packing. Aryia joined her a moment later, a wide smile on her face.

"I cannot wait to see my papa," Aryia told her. When she had trouble with the cot, Bella helped her. "Even my brothers." There was a heavy silence between them as they worked together to clear the area, knowing there was one person who wouldn't be there.

Before she knew it, they were in the air. Aryia began talking about how their planet was one covered with endless water called oceans. Bella listened to her babble, sharing more knowledge about their world than Bella thought possible for a child her age, even one as precocious as Aryia.

When they finally spotted the war ship and Draken started their ascent, Bella was both relieved and sad. They had gone on this amazing yet terrible adventure and Bella was thankful it was over, but putting it behind her meant giving up something she would miss. She tried to push the thought aside; there was too much at stake for her to focus on that.

All of those thoughts vanished when she saw Aleron waiting for them. He'd developed a beard and a haggard expression. She'd never seen her powerful brother like this. The moment they set down, Aryia was up and out the back hatch. Her niece's arms were open wide as Aleron stooped to pick her up. Bella was a little slower, letting Aryia have a moment with her father.

Suddenly Draken was beside her, wordless as he waited. She smiled up at him, realizing he was trying to comfort her in his own way. "It is moments like this that I wish Bandon were still alive. That I'd have someone waiting for me. Just me."

"They're waiting." His nodded his head toward her family.

Bella saw Aryia point back, and she knew Draken was right. Rushing from the ship, she joined them, her arms wrapping around both Aleron and Aryia as far as they could stretch. There were tears on her niece's cheeks. Aleron kissed the top of her head, welcoming her home.

"It is good to be together again," Bella replied, tears in her eyes. "I have missed you more than words can describe."

Aleron touched the side of her face. "You look so different. What has changed?"

Bella blinked in surprise, caught off guard. She stammered as the thoughts of what she and Draken had done swirled around her. How could she ever admit it?

Suddenly Draken's voice came from behind her. "She is of the Lin Bloodline."

That had seemed like so long ago that it took her a moment to realize that Aleron didn't know. How could he? It was shocking to realize that it had only been a little over a week since the crash. Everything seemed so surreal.

"Is this true?" Aleron asked, hope evident in his voice.

Bella nodded. "Yes." She lifted a hand and focused, and the air around them began to swirl. "See?"

"Some good from this tragedy." His eyes were filled with fire. "Now all I need is Azel, and the world will be right."

Hearing her name had an instantly sobering effect. Bella felt worry gnaw at her insides. Already so much time had passed—in what state would they find Azel? She felt sick at the thought.

"Do you think she's…" Aryia's voice trailed off, her entire being emanating concern.

Aleron kissed her forehead. "No, my dear child. Your mother is tough and unwieldy. Whoever took her will have no easy time containing her." There was a soft smile on his lips as he paused. "After all, who knows better than I that she is not the easiest captive?"

Chapter 23:
"Living Nightmare"

The great city of Nova did not feel like home without Azel. It felt even hollower now that Aleron had left to track down Azel's possible location. Without her brother's commanding presence, Bella found herself jumping at shadows. When sleep came, it was not restful. Now that it was over, now that she was safe behind the walls of the palace, she'd never felt more alone.

Her eyes snapped to the twins as Aryia read a book in the corner. Their corkscrew curls were pressed together as they arranged blocks on the floor. When the tower was tall enough, one would squeal as they knocked it over, the pair of them dissolving into peals of laughter before they began building again. Their merriment broke the melancholy of her thoughts.

There was a hushed knock on the door. Bella wasn't sure the sound was real until the door opened and Draken entered. They'd kept their distance, but with Aleron away, Draken was taking their security very seriously. Guards were posted everywhere, and nearly every hour on the hour, Draken made a personal stop.

"Has there been any word?" Bella asked, beginning the same dance.

"No," Draken replied curtly.

Bella didn't take it personally; she knew he had to be frustrated to have been left behind while his Liege faced unknown dangers alone. She wasn't sure what was worse, having both of them away or Aleron being alone without Draken to protect him. It might have been selfish, but she didn't want both of them to be gone.

"All is well here." Bella finished their little dance.

"Then I will return to my duties." He needed no other encouragement and took his leave.

Bella sighed before glancing back down at her embroidery. It was a depiction of Sol and Nova, the heavenly bodies of Zendar. She'd intended it as a gift for Azel's birthday, something to look forward to in these dark times, but she'd made very little progress on the moon, and the sun was only half done.

When a servant entered with a tray, Bella stood. "Shall we have lunch in the garden?"

The boys shrieked in delight, and Aryia abandoned her book. The servant nodded to her as they left the room. Two guards joined them, silent protectors in her brother's absence. The twins held each of her hands as Aryia followed. She'd been quiet and withdrawn since their return. Bella had noticed she stayed close by, as though she also felt Aleron's absence as keenly.

"Where is Papa?" Oren asked.

"He is busy finding your mama," Bella replied, trying to ignore the ache in her breast.

"I hope he comes back soon," the other twin, Ewan, said.

Bella unintentionally sighed. "I as well."

The twins were tugging on her hands and jumping when suddenly there was a loud clanking noise. Bella froze. It was the sound of two swords meeting. There was a grunt followed by a sickening slicing noise. Bella started backpedaling as the two guards surged forward. Shoving the twins toward Aryia, she herded them around the corner. She shushed them when they tried to speak as she searched for somewhere to hide them. Her hands shook badly as she attempted to open a door. It was locked.

As she propelled them down the hall, the sound of battle met her ears, followed closely by a cry that was quickly silenced. Bella tried the next door as Aryia comforted the twins and kept them silent. This one opened, and she shoved them into the room.

"Hide and stay quiet," she hissed. Then, without thought to her own safety, she closed the door between them.

Her heart in her throat and a drumming in her ears, she went to the end of the hall, back toward the attackers. The guard, the younger one, was holding his own, but he had a nasty cut on his leg and the man he faced, who was all in black, could clearly see, by the way he moved, that he wouldn't last long. Instead of facing them there, Bella dashed down the hall away from them, making her presence known. When she heard a choking sound, she glanced back as the young guard crumple into a heap.

A second man had appeared with the first, and he'd run the guard through. The sight of blood made Bella's stomach twist, but her only thought was to lead them away from the children. Once she reached the end of the passageway she went to the balcony and called for the guards in the courtyard below. Gathering her courage she turned to face the assassins. She didn't know what they were, but she knew what *she* was. Gathering her strength, she called on her powers, hand shaking and knees weak, but unwilling to back away from the living nightmares. The intruders were already advancing towards her, menace and malcontent in their posture.

"Leave!" Bella shouted, bringing her arms down.

A massive wind whooshed from behind her and barreled into them. They were thrown backward and landed hard by the lifeless bodies of the guards before skidding across the floor. Turning on her heel, she bolted down the hall to her left. She only made it a dozen steps, however, when something wrapped around her legs. Her whole body seized as she went down like a sack of vegetables.

Bella smacked her hands hard on the marble floor, stars dancing in front of her eyes. Shifting, she saw the bola wrapped around her calf and ankles. She began to yank at the leather cord, but the assassins wasted no time. Bella felt the hum of her ability but she couldn't get more than a stiff breeze, through which they walked easily.

Legs finally free, she started to crawl backward away from them, their bloodied swords a reminder of her impending fate. As they came within a few feet, one lifted his sword to deliver a blow. A scream erupted from Bella's throat as it swung down. She covered her head and rolled onto her side, tensing for death. Instead there was a thwacking noise.

Peeking out, she could see two men engaged in combat, moving away from her. Relief flooded through her as she uncurled and sat up. Gasping, Bella backed away from the dead assassin at her feet, his eyes glossy and flat.

A guard stood over her as Draken attacked the remaining assassin. For a moment, Bella was mesmerized. Draken's physical prowess was a beautiful but deadly sight to behold. He was ruthless and relentless, driving the assassin back until the man tried to flee. In the end, he was cut down and Bella watched as he collapsed. Without mercy, Draken drove his boot into the other man's head, cracking it like an egg. Part of her was disgusted by the violence and the gore, but another part remembered her own injury and the poor dead guards who'd died protecting them.

Turning back, Draken locked eyes with her, and she felt like a hare who'd been spotted by a sand viper. He stalked over, sheathing his sword as he went, before grabbing her shoulders.

"Are you hurt?" he demanded. His voice had this razor edge to it that she'd never before heard.

Her body felt like it was floating to the point she didn't have control of it. "I don't think so," Bella replied, dazed.

"Where were you thinking?" he yelled, shaking her.

"The children," Bella gasped, ignoring how angry he was and how much it cut into her. She'd been brave, the bravest she'd ever been and instead of being proud, he was furious.

His painful hold on her arm softened. "Where are they?"

"This way." When she moved toward them, he shifted to let her by.

Draken and the other guard followed. When she arrived at the room, it was locked. She knocked on the door and called out to them until the door opened. Three bawling children collapsed into her arms as she knelt to their level. She soothed them as best she could, wishing she could cry with them, but fought back the overwhelming flood of tears.

"Let's go." Draken practically hauling her to her feet and ushered them down the hall. He was yelling orders, but Bella had her hands full with three inconsolable children.

When they reached the reinforced room he set up a dozen guards, searching the room thoroughly before ordering her inside. It was a steel-clad room. It hadn't been used in a long time, but it was surprisingly clean.

"No more heroics," he snapped. "If someone comes, you go into that room and you secure it, no matter what. Do you understand?" He pointed at one of the two heavily fortified rooms that nothing could penetrate.

"Yes." With that, he was gone.

Chapter 24:
"Joined"

Bella paced the main room, worried that if she sat down she'd drift off. Inside the fortified room to her left, Aryia slept wedged between the twins. Their sweet curls and adorable faces were enough to reassure Bella when she'd put them to bed an hour before. Striding over to the balcony, Bella once more checked on the single airship that could function even at night. Barely any moonlight entered from the well-hidden alcove with the one-of-a-kind airship in case a hasty exit was needed. The other fortified room's door lay open to her right and she stared at it with mixed emotions. Despite the security the room should have brought, she only felt caged.

It had been hours since Draken had rescued her and brought them here. She was restless with the knowledge she'd nearly died. If he'd arrived a minute later, she likely would have been skewered on an assassin's blade. On the other hand, she was proud of how courageously she'd faced those men. It had been surprisingly cathartic to face them and then see them die. Instead of feeling fear or sadness, she felt invigorated. She wanted to live her life and stop being afraid. More than anything, she wanted to join her brother in the search for Azel to make their family whole again. Only then would the world be set right.

The door opened abruptly behind her, and she whirled around as the curtains beside her billowed at the surge in her powers. A click followed Draken's entry, his eyes fixed on her. She felt something there she hadn't expected—heat radiating off him. Wordlessly, she opened her arms.

In a few quick strides he wrapped her in a crushing hug. The air whooshed out of her. The relief that surged through him hit her square in the chest. He'd been so terse earlier that she'd assumed their relationship was back to where it had started. Feeling him in her arms as he buried his face against her neck told her different—this was not something the old Draken would have done.

Words were stuck on her tongue, and she was unwilling to break the moment. Instead, she clung to him with the same ferocity that he brought to his hold on her. When he finally eased back, Bella touched a hand to his cheek, reassuring him that she was alive and well. They moved in tandem, lips meeting. The tenderness lasted a few moments before he carried her to the column between the two doors and braced her against it. His kisses scorched her, burning themselves as much against her skin as into her memory.

Easing back, he studied her face. She felt bewildered, overcome by what his lips were telling her. That she mattered to him. That they were more than they had been. That every decision he'd made had been to get back to her. It swelled within her, the need and the want. She'd take whatever he was willing to give, and part of her knew it would be everything.

Tipping her head up, she felt one of his arms close around her, drawing her close. The other one wove into her hair, gripping it and the back of her head. He plundered her mouth, taking everything and giving back as much as he took. When his leather armor was rough against her, she protested, and he quickly removed the barrier. It skidded across the floor, soon forgotten as his lips trailed down her neck. He coaxed her robe open as heat pooled between her legs. He located her nipple with his mouth and then his teeth—eliciting a gasp and then a moan from her.

Fear is what had held Bella back in the past—but facing death had broken that. She was no longer afraid; she was going to get what she wanted. Her fingers gripped his hair as he plundered first one breast and then the other. She tried to stifle the noises with the back of her other hand but it was difficult.

His lips trailed down her stomach as he knelt before her. She nearly asked him what he was doing, but he nipped at her hip before sliding off her underclothing. Lifting her leg at his insistence, she knew what was coming. She braced her leg over his shoulder as her hands went over her head to grip the column, her heated flesh a stark contrast to the chilled stone. When his tongue found its mark, she arched to give him better access. He sucked and teased her as she felt pressure building. Instead of fighting it, she let it become her.

"Drake," she whispered as she lifted her other leg.

He dedicated his entire attention on the sensitive nub, and it wasn't long until she reached the highest peak, his fingers digging into her bottom as she shattered into a billion blissful pieces. Panting, she floated back down to the planet.

His eyes were impossibly dark. She took her shaking legs off his shoulders and saw him start to stand. Determined to have her way this time, she pushed against his shoulders. Off balance, he tumbled back, his hand hitting the floor as he let out an expletive under his breath.

His expression was etched in surprise when he met her gaze, but she was already lifting her robe as she straddled him. In one quick movement, she shifted the front of his pants to release his throbbing cock. It sprung free, and she glanced up at him as she wrapped her hand around its girth. He grunted and she saw his eyes close, eyebrows furrowed.

"We can't go back," he whispered as she repositioned herself.

"Who says I want to?" Bella asked boldly before droppimg her hips.

She was slick from earlier, but his head still stretched her muscles as it entered her. It felt amazing and overwhelming all at once. Gasping, she pitched forward, her hands on his chest, fingers grasping at his coarse chest hair and corded muscles. He was only partially inside of her and a part of her worried she couldn't take any more. When she glanced up at his face and saw the elation, Bella knew she would suffer worse than sore muscles to have this moment, to know the effect she was having on him.

Holding tight, she watched his face as she shifted her hips and took more of him. Her legs shook and threatened to buckle as his hands went to her hips, his fingers digging into her flesh. He muttered something about her being the death of him, which elicited a smile from her. This was unlike anything she'd ever experienced.

Suddenly, his hips moved up, and she arched in response to his full penetration. Everything was alive all at once as he held her in place, filling her to the brim and making them one. Thoughts merged into feelings, and she couldn't untangle them. When he carefully began to move out of her she gripped his thighs, overcome with each new sensation. Instead of leaving her, he immediately plunged the short distance and filled her. It elicited a cry of surprise and pleasure.

Encouraged by her reaction, he began the same motion, vigorously repeating it as he drove her higher and higher. This was so much different than earlier. She tried to grasp why, but concepts were difficult as she drowned in the passion. It brought out a carnal side of her that reveled in every thrust. Through hooded eyes, Bella locked her gaze on his. Before, she had been alone on the wave of sexual gratification, but now he was with her. Together they rode it as her control fell away and she was a feeling, wild creature, without thought or reason. All that mattered was Draken and what he was doing to her.

This time when she reached the breaking point it was like lightening through her veins. Her body clenched, her legs failed her, and her head tipped back as it washed over her. That's when she heard him groan, drawing her attention. He hastily lifted her up and twisted sideways. Startled, she nearly fell over as her sex was wet against his hip. Then she felt something hot on her leg as Draken's member brushed against her thigh. She saw the white substance spray across the floor a moment later. The expression on Draken's face was one of ecstasy.

He swore before glancing at her. As they panted, bodies slick with sweat, she worried if he'd regret what they'd done. He'd been so against it, and yet she'd wanted it. In a way, she'd forced herself on him—a bold move and so unlike her. He did that to her. She didn't know when it had changed, but they were there now.

Suddenly, he shifted and sat up. He threaded his fingers into her hair and his palm against her cheek. "Are you hurt?"

Half hope and half fear, Bella barely managed to respond around the lump in her throat. "Not at all."

<>

As she curled against him in sleep, Draken couldn't call it a mistake. It would have been too easy to call it such a thing. To label it so cruelly. To be filled with regret. Part of him was determined to censure himself for the moment of weakness, but another part, a bigger part, wanted to do it again. Wanted the sweetness she embodied. He had nearly lost her, and it had broken him more than he thought. When had she become so important to him? It had been gradual.

It complicated his plans. It was going to make everything increasingly difficult, and he didn't know how he was going to make this work. No matter what he did, Bella would be hurt. He couldn't tell her, couldn't fix it. He'd always been a solitary man—he preferred it that way. People could not be trusted. Yet here he was, the one who was a fraud. The one keeping secrets.

What was worse, she didn't suspect a thing. Bella trusted him, perhaps blindly, but that didn't change the facts. He was a no-good rotten scoundrel and she was all goodness. The secrets he bore, when they came to light, would be a betrayal. Part of him hoped it was a phase, but he suspected it was not. If she asked again, if she asked anything, he could not refuse her—could not deny what he was coming to crave for himself.

Draken shifted Bella closer against him, and she responded by snuggling against him with a contented sigh. The sweet scent of some flower wafted from her hair. Even in sleep, she told him how she felt, and he knew, without a doubt, that he was in serious trouble.

Chapter 25:
"Brave"

When Bella awoke, she was not surprised to find herself alone. Disappointed, perhaps, but not worried. There was much Draken had to attend to, and it would not wise to be caught. They'd pushed past a boundary that was usually reserved for a wife or a concubine. As she was neither to Draken, he was duty bound to make her one or the other. As a princess, Bella could not be the latter, so his only option was marriage. Being a widow and not a virgin gave her some latitude, but not much since she was still so young. Perhaps before last night her transgressions could have been forgiven, but not now. Now she was a sinful woman.

With a sigh, she rolled over, immediately regretting it when her inner thighs and feminine area reminded her of how she'd abused them last night. Groaning, she rolled back to her former position, but still the dull ache persisted. Her body had certainly enjoyed itself yesterday, but today she was paying the price. She'd gone from zero intercourse to massive penetration in short order. The thought brought a smile to her lips, and she realized she was quite keen to repeat it soon. When her body could manage a repeat performance.

Before she could dwell on it much longer, the door to the other fortified room opened. Bella drew the blanket up to her throat, realizing she was naked as the day she was born and all her clothes were still in the main room. A blush spread from her cheeks down to her toes; thankfully the room's walls were so thick that nothing they'd done the night before could have been overheard by the children or guards.

Pulling the blankets around her, Bella peeked out of the room as Aryia went to the private lavatory, rubbing at her eyes as she went. Draken had apparently draped it over the back of the closest chair right in plain view. Once Aryia disappeared behind the closed door, Bella scrambling to get dressed. She couldn't find her underclothing at first but eventually fished them out from under the lounge chair. Out of time, she balled it in her hand as Aryia reappeared, her eyes just as sleepy. Bella was thankful her niece had never been much of a morning person.

"Morning," Aryia mumbled, shuffling back toward the bedroom.

"Blessed day," Bella replied, unable to completely relax.

Bella only stopped smiling like an idiot when the door closed behind Aryia. The prospect of almost getting caught had made her temporarily forget how sore she was. The moment she was off the hook, Bella's legs turned into sponges, and she flopped onto the couch. Grunting at how hard it was, she groaned at her own stupidity.

Sighing, she stared at the limestone ceiling, wondering what the day would bring. She'd need to tell Aleron the truth at some point. The prospect didn't sit well with her. Barely were the thoughts through her mind before her stomach rumbled. She glanced around, remembering she didn't have any other clothes. She could have servants take care of both, but she didn't want to stay in the room. She needed to stretch her legs, and her belongings weren't far—close enough that she could be back in the blink of an eye.

After wriggling into her underclothing, she went to the children's door and tested it. It was locked, and she felt a swell of pride at Aryia still being aware enough to lock it behind her. Assured that the children were boxed in and safe, Bella tried to comb her hair with her fingers as she adjusted her robe.

She opened the door and walked out like she owned the place. Her bare feet made almost no noise on the polished marble. There were multiple guards posted around the area, including one she recognized, Nitya's husband, Ramas, who was at the end of the hall talking with another guard. He was tall, with a head of thick black hair, and kind eyes. Bella had been introduced to him when Nitya had become Azel's principal handmaiden. Nitya was not of the Bloodlines, but Ramas was a child of Imoten, with his hard skin. It made him an ideal defender.

"Princess," said the guard right outside her door, "the General commanded you remain here and safe."

That drew Ramas's attention. She acknowledged him with a nod of her head before addressing the man who'd spoken to her. "The children and I will need clothing before breakfast is brought to me."

"Princess." He appeared uncomfortable. "General Draken was specific in my orders. You were not to leave. I can send for a servant."

Normally, Bella would have crumbled in the face of conflict and a direct order from Draken. This time she lifted herself up and met the guard's stare. "Were the room I sought across the palace, I would be inclined to agree." She nodded ahead. "My room is barely a moment away, and the children's a few doors down. I'd prefer to stretch my legs and gather them myself." She could see the panic in his eyes. "I will most assuredly will take a personal escort."

Emboldened by recent events, Bella didn't wait for a reply and started down the hall. The guards shuffled uncomfortably, but it was Ramas who eventually stepped into her path. He didn't appear nervous, but he was quizzical.

"Where are you going, Princess?"

"To my room," Bella replied, taking a step forward.

Ramas took a step back to keep pace with her. "I can request that someone retrieve your clothing."

"I'd prefer to go myself," Bella fixed him with her best royal stare before taking another step. He kept pace with her.

"We have orders."

Bella suppressed the urge to sigh. "As I told the other guard, I'll take an escort, but you will not stop me."

This time she barreled ahead, no longer amused or patient. She was standing in the middle of the hall in clothes only family would be permitted to see her in. Given the circumstances, this would be overlooked, but it was grating against her. Suddenly her newfound strength let her see that sometimes it was better to ignore orders.

Ramas followed as she strode down the hall. She could hear the jingle of his armor and the soft shuffle of his boots. She was quickly to her door.

"You can wait here," Bella told him, pleased with her defiance.

Before the words were out of her mouth, he was shaking his head. "Let me clear the room." Ramas drew his sword and went across the threshold.

Crossing her arms, she sighed heavily; acting as though she was in charge was quite draining. Her mind wandered to the night before. She felt so different and yet the same. Altered, that was the word she'd been searching for.

Suddenly the door at the end of the hall—the room Aleron was in while Azel was missing—opened. He'd wanted to be closer to the rest of the family so he'd had the rooms prepared. Startled, she turned, expecting to see a servant or her brother himself. Instead, Draken appeared.

Baffled, she called to him, "Draken?" Torn between happiness and confusion she asked, "Is my brother back?"

His head snapped around and his brows furrowed. "What are you doing here? Where are the guards?"

As if on cue, Ramas appeared. "I am here, General."

"Why is she here?" Draken demanded. "I gave you an order."

"Well, I countermanded it," Bella interjected as she took another step toward the room. "You did not answer my question. Is my brother here?"

"No, the Liege is still gone," Draken replied, then flicked an angry glare at Ramas. "You may return."

Ramas bowed. "General."

Bella didn't wait for him to leave. "Then why were you in his room?"

"It is none of your concern." The words were harsh, impersonal.

Bella felt the sting of them against her face—as though they'd slapped her. She blinked back the shock, trying to gain her bearings. He was keeping something from her. The realization cut deep. She'd thought they'd come so far, and yet still there were secrets between them. Her own, the fact that she likely couldn't have children, heavy on her mind.

Upset and not willing to show it, she hurried into the room. Finding simple slippers first, she quickly turned her attention to hastily gathering some clothes. Then she went to the children's rooms, one by one, gathering items for them. Every time she left he was standing there, waiting for her, but she refused to look at him and let him see how much he'd hurt her.

Her arms were heaping and she had a bag over each shoulder when she emerged the final time. Draken moved toward her as though to help, but she sidestepped and rushed past him. Without looking back, Bella marched her way back to the rooms. She heard him following behind her, and a part of her knew she was reacting in a childish way.

An even bigger part, though, the part that was winning, didn't care because he'd wounded her.

When she reached the room, the men were much more rigid than they'd been earlier. Instantly feeling the difference, Bella sensed what had changed. She hurried toward the room and shouldered through the door. When she saw Aleron with his children, her heart clenched. She tossed the clothing on the closest chair, dumped the bags on the floor and ran to him.

"Bella." Aleron smiled at her, the first genuine smile she'd seen in days. "I wondered where you'd gotten off to."

"To get clothes." Bella hugged him, grateful he was safe. "What news do you have?"

"I found her," Aleron replied, glancing at those around him. "She has been taken back to Undel."

Bella felt her heart sink, remembering what Titus had done to his and Azel's father. "Back to where it all began."

Aleron nodded. "Yes. And I need your help."

"Anything." Bella glanced at the children, who were all transfixed by their conversation. "Anything to make our family whole."

He touched a hand to her cheek. "You have become so brave."

Bella felt her eyes drawn to the door where Draken was standing. Their eyes met, and Bella felt a tightness in her chest. "I have to be."

Chapter 26:
"A Fall"

Bella's hand shook as they stood on the airship overlooking Undel. Like all of the Bloodline cities, this one was built upon a massive plateau above Zendar's sandy landscape. The glass was so clean and clear that she felt she would pitch forward to her death. The city rose up behind the palace as she approached the meeting location. A small army was gathered on the landing area as they slowly swept past. Her fingers tightened around the child's hand. Aleron had been sure this would work, but Bella couldn't shake the sense of foreboding as they prepared to land.

"You're hurting me," Verik said, drawing her attention.

They were expecting Aryia, but instead they would get a boy. At six and eight years old, it was difficult to tell boys and girls apart. Their voices were difficult to distinguish, and Verik was no exception. In fact, Bella was convinced that boys shrieked more than girls. He even wore his hair longer to emulate Aleron, so with it styled femininely, it was challenging to tell what gender he was.

She very much doubted Titus knew what Aryia looked like, and they only had to trick him long enough to get Azel out. If everything had gone according to plan Aleron was already in the castle, or so she hoped. Bella tried to remain calm as they landed beside the royal ship. Knowing that Aryia was far away in the city of Sol under Hadish's protection brought her, at least, some degree of comfort.

Still holding Verik's hand, Bella made her way to the opening at the back of the vessel. The solar-powered wings glinted in the setting sun as she reached the hatch. The ship jolted, and Bella wobbled. Verik almost fell down, but they were able to recover as the guard loosened the chains. The back dropped open as the ship settled, and Bella felt ill with dread.

A man out front, his hands on his hips, glared at them. "Who do we have here?" She knew without a doubt that he was Titus, Azel's brother and a traitor.

Squaring her shoulders, Bella marched down the gangplank with as much grace as she could muster. “I am Azobella Corvinus, princess to the Cities of Sol and Nova, sister to the mighty Liege Aleron and his queen Azel, daughter and princess of Undel. I demand you release her at once.”

There was pause as she stepped out onto the rooftop. The guards assigned to their protection remained behind her on the ship. After a moment, Titus and his men burst out laughing, and Bella struggled to remain impassive as she was unnerved by their blatant mockery.

Titus unsheathed his sword. “I’ll release her all right. Where is Aleron?” He snarled the words. Bella swallowed hard as Verik pressed in tighter to her side.

“Aboard a second ship that will land on the opposite side,” Bella replied, pointing to the ship a good distance away.

“Ah, you won’t face me together.” Titus waved a hand. “I had hoped to do this with Aleron present to watch his wife suffer, but I’ll take her daughter watching.”

The venom in his voice made Bella’s blood run cold. Knots formed in her stomach as three bound and hooded women were pushed forward and forced onto their knees. Titus stood behind them. Bella prayed to Zendar that her brother would hurry. They were running out of time!

Bella marshaled up all her false bravado. “I have all the might of the army to face you.”

“All I see is a scared, powerless girl.” Titus laughed. “Even if you had powers, they’d be useless.”

Apparently she was better known than she thought. Powerless royalty didn’t happen often, on the other hand, and were the bane of a family. “I will take Aryia and leave if you don’t release Azel.”

Titus ignored her as three guards made their way down. “Who is up first?” Titus jerked one of the hoods off, revealing a crying woman too tall and thin to be Azel. “Sister Zena, lucky number one.” Bella had only seen Azel’s sister a few times, but she was almost unrecognizable in her current state.

He moved so quickly that Bella didn’t have time to protest. The dagger’s tip ripped through her body. One of the other women yanked off her own hood, revealing Azel’s gaunt but determined face. She had a gag across her mouth. She pitched forward to help Zena as she writhed on the floor, but one of Titus's men grabbed hold of her.

Why wasn't she using her power?

The guards on the gangplank of the airship moved forward in defense of their Queen, but Titus put a dagger against Azel's throat. "Stay back."

Bella was torn to pieces by watching Zena gasp in pain, clasping her side where the blade had cut. When she groaned too loudly, Titus kicked her. Then he went around and knelt in front of Azel, who had stopped squirming. Bella held her breath, searching for any sign of rescue. Where was her brother? Frantic but frozen, she watched in horror as Titus snagged the bottom of Azel's face. Verik buried his face against her side but Bella forced herself to keep looking.

"Powerless to save her. Now you know how it feels." Titus's words were so soft that she could barely hear them. "And you will know what it is like to lose what you love most." Titus stood and turned. "Get them."

A knife flew into the neck of one of the guards. Blood bubbled out of his mouth and down his chin as he fell to his knees. Horrified, Bella shifted Verik back behind her. The other guards surged forward.

"Run!" Azel screamed around the gag.

The sound of her voice broke Bella's trance. Bella yelled for the ship to take off and was halfway up the ramp when something wrapped around her arms. The rope tightened as it jerked her back away from Verik's hand. She landed hard and felt fear sweep in. Like a thunderclap, her power exploded off her. Rolling onto her side, she jerked the bindings off and let them drop. Men were getting to their feet, and Azel's eyes were wide with surprise. Titus stood in front of her, unfazed. His sword was back in his hand in a flash. Bella turned back in time to see the ship lift with Verik inside. Relief and fear mixed together as she dashed toward it.

She jumping toward the open back as a guard moved toward her. When Verik called for the ship to go down, she screamed at them to leave her. She knew what would become of Verik if the boy was caught, and her guards were falling one by one. When the ship tried to stop, she let her power free a second time and thrust the ship forward, propelling it safely away. It dipped and chipped out a section of the edge of the roof as Bella stopped where the wall rose up from the room. The end of the line, the only place to go was down.

When she turned around, she saw Titus bleeding from a cut on his face, his lips in a furious snarl. He moved toward her, but the others hesitated. Bella shifted her back leg toward the edge of the palace's roof, preparing to jump off and use her ability to land on the rock face of the plateau below. Despite the option for escape, she felt it was wrong to leave. Azel was still in harm's way, and Zena was injured, perhaps dying.

"I'll tear you limb from limb," Titus growled.

Before she could decide what to do, there was a battle cry. A group drove against the men like a well-aimed spear. Bella stood frozen as Titus and his men surged against the unexpected attack in an attempt to regain control.

Heart in her throat, Bella watched the chaos, saw the way the blood wet the sand and stone, and heard the cries of the fallen. Her eyes were drawn to Aleron and Draken as they carved their way through the men. Their lethalness outweighed all others.

Holding her breath Bella saw Titus and Aleron moving towards Azel, who was crawling toward her husband. With a muted clang, Aleron's and Titus's blades met. As they traded blows, Draken lifted Azel and carried her back toward the safety of their line. Titus was fury itself as he tried to press Aleron back—shouting 'no' multiple times, as though words could injure her mighty brother.

Aleron sidestepped, meeting him again. Suddenly, a second man joined fight, so that Aleron was defending himself against two men. Bella noticed a man coming about a dozen feet away, walking toward her. Without thinking, she stepped backward, and then she was off the edge, the side of the building sweeping up past her and her hair whipping around her face. The cliffs greeted her below as she tried to calm her mind enough to harden the air and slow her fall.

Bella felt it stiffen and slow her descent, but then something flew past her, breaking her concentration. She looked up to see a man with a crossbow leaning over the edge. With a scream she tried to stop herself again, but this time her focus was entirely concentrated on her right side, which sent her spinning off to the left. After a moment, the ground rushing up to meet her, she tried again. She was able to slow herself enough that she landed on her feet, but she fell to the side from the force of the impact.

Her entire left side screamed at her. The air had been knocked out of her, and tears sprang to her eyes. With a groan, she rolled to her back, struggling to inhale. She'd made a mess of it. New to her Bloodline, Bella had jumped in feet first, insisting to Aleron she was ready.

Tears of pain turned to bitter disappointment in herself. Not knowing if her family was safe made the world seem unbearable. Bandon's death had sucker-punched her stomach, leaving her reeling. What if she lost Draken too?

Then it hit her—she was in love with Draken. The realization swirled around her, strangling her with apprehension. Once she caught her breath and sat up, some of the shame passed. In its stead was a need to find out the fate of her family and of the man she loved. Standing, she dusted off her clothing. One side of her skirt had torn and was hanging limply on the ground. Leaning down, she tore the rest of it away.

"I can do this," Bella whispered to herself.

Cautiously she concentrated on the space in front of her. She tried to harden a set of stairs. One foot at a time she scaled it, but instead of something firm like rock, it was as yielding as sand, shifting under her feet. When she reached the top, she was breathing hard from the effort. Head tilted back, she stared at the massive faceless wall rising up before her in all its intimidating glory.

The closest window was far above her head, and although Bella felt brave, she wasn't stupid. Instead, she evaluated the steep incline to her right. Carefully, she made her way to the left and peeked around the corner. The wind rushed against her face, blowing her hair in every direction. Glancing up, she could make out a lower window but it was further up the rock face, where the wind was buffeting against the walls. The ledge narrowed and below was the rugged cliff. One slip, and she might not have a chance to recover.

Making up her mind, she stepped out, her skirts flaring around her as unyielding wind slapped against her. Zendar was hot and humid, but the ferocity behind the gusts of air made the day feel frigid. Despite that, she pressed on, determined to get back to her family. She felt tears prick her eyes, but she refused to be overcome by fear.

She clung to the rock face and let out a yelp as the wind buffeted against her back. Fear surfaced, and she was certain she would fall to her death despite her Bloodline. As though called forth, her ability swirled around her, fighting back against the relentless assault. A pocket of protection formed around her, and it steeled her resolve.

Above her, the window was close but a good distance up—at least thrice her height. If she missed, it could mean a further fall. It was a risk she couldn't afford, but it was one she had to take. Focusing, she bent her legs and bounced a few times, forcing herself to try. She stopped and leaned her head against the wall, scared out of her mind. Then she had an idea.

Concentrating on the air, she hardened it. Again it was like sand, not hard like rock, but she was able to begin scaling it like a ladder. Refusing to look down or up, she just focused on climbing. Sweat broke out on her brow from the effort, exhaustion seeping into her arms as she ascended. Just as she was sure she couldn't go another step, the ledge came into view. Hauling herself up, she practically fell into the room.

It was a storehouse for clothing. Linens lined the walls with a few hanging from hooks and lines. The breeze sweeping through the massive window made them dance as Bella searched for a door. The moment she spotted it, her legs carried her to and through it. The next room was empty but appeared to be a cleaning room, with big floor tubs for washing. Room after room, stairs after stairs, she moved as quickly as she could.

When the decor became more opulent, Bella knew she must be close to the throne room or at least the royal apartments. Disoriented and with a sense of panic rising in her chest, she nearly screamed when she rounded a corner and saw a guard. It took her a few seconds to realize that it wasn't actually a guard but rather a statue. Chiding herself for being so ridiculous, Bella hurried on, wondering why the hallways were so deserted.

She turned a corner and saw blood splattered across the floor. It didn't take Bella long to spot the crumpled body. His glassy eyes and a massive gash told her he wasn't alive. Heart hammering in her chest, she quickly passed, careful to step around the blood.

The sound of muffled voices came from the distance. She tracked the sounds, hoping they would lead her to Azel or Aleron or even Draken—anyone who could tell her what had happened. As she rounded another corner she saw a group of Undel's and Nova's guards outside in the hallway. One spotted her immediately.

The Undel soldier held his sword at the ready. "State your name and purpose."

The soldier next to him, a woman wearing Nova's standard, pushed his sword down. "That is Princess Bella." Her voice reminded her of the metal brush on the cast-iron pots. "Lower your sword, you fool."

"Where are they?" Bella demanded, eager to see them.

The female guard needed no further explanation on who Bella was inquiring after. "They are dispatching justice." She swept back and held the door open for her.

"Thank you," Bella replied, hurrying toward the door.

Inside, she could see a host of guards around the dais. At its steps was Azel, now wrapped in Aleron's fine cloak. Aleron stood with two swords held at the throat of a man who was now barely recognizable as Titus. A busted eye and blood covered his face, his hair was matted, and he had a nasty gash across his chin. Their powers might not work on him, but Aleron didn't need his powers to defeat his opponents; he was a superb swordsman.

"Your sorrows have been great." Azel's sarcastic words cut through the room like a knife. "You betrayed our father. Had my mother killed. Stabbed our sister." Bella crept along the wall, most the guards not noticing her. Those who did nodded to her. "I should visit every pain upon you."

"You took from me what was mine!" Titus's voice was still full of spite. "You and that devil of a daughter."

There was general shift in the room and now Bella could feel the hatred. They were speaking of a princess of Nova, Sol, and Undel. Every solider in the room who was even partially loyal to Aleron or Azel wanted blood. From the way Aleron was standing, poised to cut off Titus's head, Bella felt they were going to get it. Bella quickly surmised that Draken wasn't in the room.

When Azel spoke next, she sounded tired, almost sad. "Though you do not deserve it, I will grant you a mercy you denied our father."

Titus's expression was guarded. "What is that?"

"A quick death."

Aleron moved so quickly that Bella only saw the blood on his swords, the crimson lifeblood dripping onto the pale limestone floor. A moment later, Titus's body slumped back and his head rolled away, coming to rest at the bottom of the stairs. A guard stepped forward and picked up the head, staring at his Liege expectantly.

A glance deferred the decision to Azel. "Place his head and body on a spike for all of Undel to see. To see what becomes of traitors."

There was a general cheer before several people, mostly from Undel, moved to retrieve his body. Aleron and Azel remained unmoving until there were few people left. Aleron gathered Azel against him in an open show of affection. Many of those who remained averted their gaze and shuffled out. Bella did not. Bella strode forward, pleased to see both Aleron and Azel well and wanting to be close to them.

Aleron's head came up when he saw her, and he immediately opened his other arm. Azel tipped her head back and Bella saw genuine happiness. Tears immediately sprung to Bella's eyes, and an unintentional sob escaped her throat. She barreled headfirst against them, and they laughed and patted her back.

"I missed you," she gurgled, clinging to Azel like a child.

"It is good to be missed," Azel replied. "It is even better to be free."

"And so you shall remain," Aleron replied. "I am proud of you, Bella. You were strong today."

Azel framed her face while they were protected in Aleron's fold. "I had no idea you had such power. You surprised me as much as those men."

"Aryia helped me. I still can't control it." Bella blubbered.

Azel's expression changed instantly at the mention of her daughter. "Since my daughter is further away then I first thought, I want to see her and my boys." She eyed Aleron as she spoke, apparently having already clarified it was Verik and not Aryia earlier.

"I told you I would never risk our daughter," Aleron replied, his eyes sharp. "Verik has begun to train and can protect himself. Aryia is too young…and cannot." A silent understanding passed between Azel and Aleron of which Bella guessed its nature to be about Aryia's unique gift.

"Perhaps it is time we changed our ways," Azel replied, gazing over Bella's shoulder at the splattering of blood. "I have had enough of Undel. I am ready to return home."

The door creaked open behind them and drew their attention. "My Liege, I have searched the outer wall…" Draken stood on the threshold, his expression hard until he saw Bella.

Relief flooded through her as his eyebrows lifted a moment before settling back down—she'd surprised him. Proud of how she'd made it back all by herself, Bella straightened her spine and stepped out of Aleron's reach. Beaming, she practically skipped down the stairs.

"I'm glad you are well," Bella replied, feeling suddenly shy at knowing Aleron and Azel were watching. "I am glad we are all safe."

Azel eyed her for a moment before she leaned into Aleron, her arm going around his waist as they came down the steps. "Aleron, take me home."

Chapter 27:
"Enemies Abound"

Bella paced at breakfast, worried Aleron and Azel wouldn't be joining her. Once Azel had seen to Zena and her family had been secured, they'd all departed for home. Bella had gone straight to bed on the ship, exhausted from the evening's trials. Titus was dead, and it was finally over. Better yet, despite a nasty cut on her neck and the lack of good food, Azel seemed to be mostly unaffected. Their family was finally whole.

It was the wrong time to try to sort through her feelings around Draken, but now that Azel was back, it swirled around her anyway. She had loved him before, but now it was something…more. Despite Draken's insistence that lust and love were hard to differentiate, she knew it wasn't that. Well, it wasn't *only* that. It was the way he made her feel—both protected and wild, like she could do anything if he was there to catch her. Her fear and caution went to the wind, and she just *was*. He'd brought that out in her. Even before the change in their relationship, she'd felt comfortable around him, like she could be honest with him about anything. Her pain and grief over Bandon, the fear she'd experienced and the need to be held, and her desire to be with him in a more intimate way. No one else stirred such frankness from her.

Soon they would be landing at home, and Bella was going to have to come clean. The question was, should she broach it with Aleron first or Draken? Both were daunting prospects that could end very badly. Aleron could attack Draken or dismiss him, though she doubted he would kill him. What scared her more was Draken rejecting her. He'd made himself quite clear, but she couldn't believe after the night they'd spent together and how he'd been toward her that he didn't care for her. Then again, she remembered the way he'd kept secrets from her—cutting her out of whatever was happening.

Resigned, she collapsed onto a plush seat at the table. There was a hearty spread, in which she knew she should have been partaking.

Instead it sat untouched, as it had for the last quarter of an hour. They were due home soon.

Suddenly, the door opened and Bella straightened, an expectant feeling in her belly. Instead of either Azel or Aleron, it was Verik. He looked hesitant, but when he saw she was alone he perked up. Unlike Aryia, Verik seemed to enjoy the mornings.

"Good morn!" Verik told her as he sat directly to her left, despite there being five different open seats all around her.

"Good morning," Bella replied with a half smirk she tried to stifle as he started to fill his plate. "I'm glad to see you well rested after all the excitement yesterday."

Talking around a roll he'd just taken a bite of, he said, "It was so exciting!" His wide eyes shone with excitement. "Father has never asked my help for anything."

Despite caring for Le'Roy and Verik, it was still strange that Azel was so accepting of Aleron's bastard children. No other Queen as far as Bella knew had allowed the concubines to live, let alone permitted their offspring to remain within the palace. In their hour of need, Verik had helped come to her rescue, had kept Aryia safely away by acting as a stand in, which had helped delay Titus long enough for Aleron to execute his plan. Though he hadn't done much, his willingness to help their family was a sure sign that Azel had done the right thing all those years ago.

"I'm proud of you," Bella said before ruffling his hair.

When he smiled, she noticed he was missing a tooth. It made his expression almost comically adorable. "I did good, huh?" Verik seemed suddenly shy, but she could tell he was pleased.

"Very good," Bella confirmed before partaking in the food.

They ate in silence for a few minutes, just enjoying the cuisine. "Do you think I'll get to see Aryia soon?"

When they'd returned, Aleron had taken their children straight to Azel. Everyone had been sent away while the royal family spent time together. Bella would join them later, and take Verik along. Bella was happy that Aryia and Verik were so close. He was one of the few people with whom Aryia really seemed to connect.

"I am sure, now that everything is…resolved."

"I miss her. I wish I'd told her that she's my friend and that I love her while I had the chance." Verik sighed heavily for an eight-year-old before returning to his drink.

Bella stared at Verik, shocked by his straightforward honesty. He'd laid it all bare in a matter of moments and without hesitation. The unfiltered consciousness that children seemed to inherently have reminded her that stating the obvious was often the best course. The gears in her head began turning, and she considered the best step forward. Perhaps she had been wrong before; perhaps now was exactly the right time.

The door opened, and Bella was startled as Aleron entered. He smiled when he saw them together. "Azel is still resting."

Verik was grinning from ear to ear. "Good morning!"

"Blessed day." Aleron patted his head before he took his seat.

"Blessed day," Bella mumbled, glancing at her mostly empty plate. In a few bites she finished what remained and announced, "I'm done eating. I believe I'll rest as well until we arrive."

"You did well," Aleron told her and she swelled with pride, more certain than ever that she had to take action.

"Thank you, brother," Bella replied before hurrying from the room.

Once outside, she wasn't sure where to begin her search for Draken. It was a smaller ship, though, and there were only so many places she could find him. Servants and guards tipped their head and she looked around, and a few called greetings that she returned. He wasn't in the guard's quarters or the general dining area. As she headed to the main controls of the ship, Bella saw him at the end of the hall talking with another guard.

Her heart in her throat, she nearly bolted into the closest room when the guard saw her. Then Draken turned his head, still speaking, until his eyes rested on her. Wide eyed, Bella held her breath for his reaction. He simply nodded his head and returned to the conversation. After a moment, the other man left.

Bella hurried to catch up to Draken's long strides. "Drake."

His glanced down at her over his shoulder. "Yes, princess?"

The formality nearly stopped her in her tracks. "I'd like to talk to you…if you have a moment." Her voice sounded small and weak to her ears, but she couldn't muster a resounding command.

"Does it need my urgent attention?" He didn't even look at her.

She hesitated. "Well, no, but it is important."

"Now isn't a good time," Draken replied quickly. "We are preparing to land in Nova."

Disheartened, Bella watched him go. Her stomach in knots, her earlier excitement and determination drained out of her. When he reached the hallway junction, he glanced back at her. The distance seemed to open a gulf between them, as though it represented how far removed he was from her emotionally. It was the first time she'd ever felt alone in his presence.

He averted his gaze after a few moments and then left. She stayed where she was, staring at the spot he'd just occupied. Perhaps he was just distant because he had duties to attend to. Perhaps it was nothing.

The niggling feeling in the pit of her stomach disagreed, but she tried her best to ignore it. The words needed to be spoken, so she would try again. In the meantime, she wanted to see Azel. She would have to be awake soon, since they were so close to Nova.

The ship dipped down as she approached Azel's rooms. There were two guards, each focused on her as she rounded the corner. A maid exited the room and came toward Bella, who stared at her in confusion. She knew all of Azel's attendants, but she'd never seen this woman before. Her hair was dark, cut shorter than was common. For a moment she wondered if the woman was from Undel, and then she saw the marking on her neck—brand Burtanians used for thieves and privateers.

The woman's eyes narrowed as she followed Bella's gaze. Bella let out a shout and flung a wild surge of wind against her, but to Bella's shock, she parted the blast of air and redirected it, slamming it into the guards. Bella stumbled backward, narrowly using her ability to cushion her fall as she landed onto her backside with a grunt.

A moment later, the guards went rushing by her, yelling at the woman to stop. The ship jostled as it landed. Dazed, Bella stumbled toward the door, her guts twisted into knots. Inside was dim, the curtains drawn against the blinding sun. The edges of light peeked in, casting a soft glow in the room.

She hurried toward the second door and she opened it to find Azel unmoving on the bed, her arms bound above her head. Bella felt tears of relief sting when she saw the rise and fall of Azel's chest. Then confusion followed. If Titus was dead, who was attacking them? Who was that woman? Were they still in danger?

She tried shaking Azel awake. "Please," she said, her words edged in desperation. "Please wake up."

When Azel didn't rise, Bella tried working on the restraints on Azel's wrists. They were like those she'd previously seen on Azel—ones that suppressed her gift. Clearly there were more enemies aboard, but who were they? Hands shaking, half blinded by tears, Bella desperately searched for anything she could use. She tried to use the back of one of Azel's earrings, but it was too thin. Then she tried a nail file, but it was too wide. Sniffling, Bella felt hopeless until she remembered she could harden air.

Bending the earring into a flat line Bella focused on it, using it as the spine of a key, before carefully inserting it into the lock. Imagining it to be metal, filling the space, Bella tried turning it but felt it twist too easily. Gritting her teeth, she repeated the effect. A smaller space was much easier to harden than a series of steps, though it still took a toll. This time when she turned it, there was a soft clicking sound.

"Yes!" Bella cheered as she pushed the first shackle off.

Azel jerked, and then something slammed against her side. Bella felt the air go right out of her as she stumbled back, dropping the earring as she clasped her side. Azel was up on her feet and had produced a knife out of nowhere, brandishing it in defense.

Azel had kneed her in the ribs! Gasping, she barely managed, "Azel it's me. It's Bella!"

The fury lessened on Azel's face and then softened. "Bella. What are you doing here? What happened?" She lifted her arm and shook the remaining manacle.

"There was a woman." Bella was still struggling to catch her breath from Azel's well-placed strike.

"A servant?" Azel sounded far away, and then she was helping Bella to her feet. "I remember a new servant brought me breakfast. Where are we?"

Bella went to the window. "We've landed in Nova." She'd recognize the whiter marble of those walls anywhere.

There was a shout outside, and the outer door banged open. In a flash, Azel barreled toward the door. Bella was a bit slower. Someone pushed against the door as Azel tried to close it. When Azel cried out her name, Bella found herself against the door, too, in an instant.

"These confounded shackles!" Azel shouted, her back against the door. They were losing ground.

Outside, someone commanded they break it down. Bella's heart was in her throat as she realized Azel couldn't help them. But *she* could.

An arm appeared in the gap. The air became heavy and in a big whoosh, Bella's gift slammed against the door. The man that the arm belonged to cried out and retracted it as Azel stumbled back and closed it, sealing off their enemies—for now.

Panting, Azel smiled up at her. "I'm so proud of you."

Beaming with pride, Bella helped Azel to her feet. "I'm getting better every day."

Azel put a hand to Bella's cheek. "You are of the Bloodline. I always felt it within you."

"Really? Why didn't you tell me?" Bella was surprised.

Something banged against the reinforced door, making her jump.

"I wasn't sure if it was strong enough," Azel replied, eyeing the door. "Now is not the time, though. Think you can get us out the window?"

Bella eyed it. "I can certainly try."

They made it two steps when the door behind them exploded. The force slammed her against the ground, her head rebounding off the floor. Ears ringing, Bella couldn't get her bearings. Wind slapped against her face as she tried to move. Disoriented, she felt someone grab her. Bella blindly tried to wrench herself away, but the person was stronger. Someone bound her wrists as her head lolled back. The world was existing in flashes, like fragmented shards. In between was blackness, a comforting release and terrifying emptiness all at once. The war waged until the darkness won.

Chapter 28:
"Family is Everything"

When Bella came to, she was on the ground. Someone was talking, but it was muffled. Someone else had a hand on her shoulder, and she could feel their comforting heat against her back. Her sense of smell returned first. Azel's scent swirled around her, and she knew it was none other than her sister by marriage that protected her.

Azel's voice cut through the throbbing in her head. "I demand to know on whose authority you've taken us prisoner."

"You will know soon enough," a gruff voice responded.

Stirring, Bella realized they were in the throne room in Nova. When she shifted, Azel did as well. "Bella?"

With a groan, Bella was helped into a sitting position by Azel. "What happened?"

"We're being held hostage," Azel replied. Then, louder, she asked, "I demand to see the Liege."

"I do not recognize your government." The voice belonged to an older man with gray streaking through his brown hair. He was dressed like a privateer, or at least how Bella imagined they would dress—leather and a plethora of weapons.

"Where is my husband?" Azel commanded. The thought of something happening to Aleron made Bella sick, but Azel's voice was demanding and without emotion. Powerful, unyielding Azel was the one person she'd wanted to be beside.

There was the sound of boots on the ground. Azel sat up straighter, as did Bella by extension, since her arms were still around her. Aleron had blood on his scalp and a metal collar around his neck. The chains connected to his wrists and ankles. Four guards held them taunt, and they jangled sinisterly.

Bella's stomach lurched as they brought her brother down on one knee. There was a tapping noise, like heels on stone. A moment later Lycin, Draken's sister, entered with a strange man on her arm. Confused, Bella's mind tried to grasp at the truth. Behind them was an opulently dressed Le'Roy and an uncomfortable Verik.

"How kind of you to join us," Lycin said with a soft but biting smile.

"Lycin," Aleron growled. "What is the meaning of this?"

"This," Lycin snapped, her face contorted into an ugly sneer. "This is a new beginning." She held a hand up and gestured Le'Roy over. "Come, son, and take your proper place."

Le'Roy went to his mother, sparing a hesitant glance in Aleron's direction. "Yes, mother."

"You see," Lycin went on, "the world needs a king who is not tainted by the blood of our enemies. One of the pure Bloodlines." A sharp glare was sent in Azel's direction. "A world free of Azel's influence. Once you told me you would conquer the world, Aleron. Now you are content to rule half of it."

Lycin had Le'Roy sit upon the throne, and she turned with a hand on his shoulder. The other man stepped forward and put a hand on Le'Roy's other shoulder. He was handsome in a roguish sort of way. His hair was cut short, which was not as often seen these days, and there was an angry scar on his forehead. His skin was darker, closer to that of the Sand People, and yet he carried himself like a man of a noble house.

"We will not be content," the man said. "We will begin here, and then all of Zendar shall be ours."

"Who are you?" Azel asked, her voice surprisingly calm and in complete contrast to the expression of revulsion on her face. "You who speaks to the Liege with such certainty."

"I am Yevik," he said with a lazy smile. "Lover of the beautiful and cunning Lycin." He held a hand out to her, and she dipped her head in reverence. Then he put his hands on Verik's shoulders. The boy's eyes were wide and cast to the side. "And father to Verik."

Bella was shocked. The whole room was deadly silent at that confession. She'd always thought Verik had seemed different from Le'Roy but had assumed he'd taken more after his mother. Scrutinizing the pair of them standing together, she could see the shape of his face and their identical noses. Despite the feeling that she should protest, Bella could believe the truth of his words.

"I know it is difficult to comprehend." Lycin chuckled to herself. "A lowly concubine betraying you, but you never treated us well.

Leaving us to be cruel to each other, only short of killing ourselves to win your affection. In the hope of becoming your queen." Her face broke into a jeer that terrified Bella. "Instead you choose her! A daughter of our sworn enemy."

Aleron scoffed. "You could never be a queen."

"I would have been great!" Lycin replied, fire in her eyes. "I knew Nova's and Sol's people. We could have washed the rest of Zendar in blood and remade this world. Instead you chose our enemy—her."

"The fighting had to end." Azel spoke up for the first time. Her words were the hallmark of a true queen—she didn't speak in defense of herself, but for Zendar.

"That is where you are wrong!" Lycin came toward them. "Your foolish brother at least knew that much. Even if he didn't know our true plan and served only to keep you preoccupied, he at least agreed that peace breeds weakness."

Suddenly, the doors opened behind Aleron. Draken entered with a group of guards. Bella felt her heart swell, certain their salvation had arrived. She held her breath when Draken went toward the dais. No one reacted; no one moved to stop him. Bella was on her feet before she knew what she was doing.

Her shirt snagged on something and she glanced back. Azel shook her head, her eyes sad. Bella felt her heart drop. She couldn't believe it, couldn't grasp what she was seeing.

"Brother." Lycin opened her arms, and Bella's legs felt unsteady. "You did well to subdue Aleron. Yevik did not think it could be accomplished."

"It is done," Draken replied, and it was like a punch to her stomach.

"Have the preparations been made?" Lycin asked.

Betrayal, hot and unforgiving, laced up Bella's body. It burned deep within her soul, marring it. She felt herself sink to the ground in shock, her mind finally comprehending but not accepting. She couldn't cry or think. Bella wanted to flee, but nothing would listen to her. Instead she was trapped.

When Draken spoke, Bella's heart shattered. "They have."

"Wonderful!" Lycin replied, giddy with excitement. "It is time we reminded Nova of what a true Corvinus of a pure Bloodline can do. Zendar will be remade."

Bella was vaguely aware of being ordered to her feet. Her eyes were fixed on Draken as she and Azel were marched behind Aleron. When she passed him, Bella flinched at the torment in his gaze. She knew beyond a shadow of a doubt that he'd betrayed her—condemning them all.

"Why?" she whispered.

When a guard tried to push her along, Draken held up a warning hand. She longed for an excuse, something to explain away what was happening. Her heart hammered and she felt lightheaded, but still she stared, expectantly.

It was he who averted his gaze first. "I'm sorry. Family is everything."

Chapter 29:
"Secrets and Truths"

Bella was jostled against Azel as they emerged in the courtyard. Her heart scattered like mirror fragments behind her with every step. There was an immediate noise from onlookers, but it barely registered. Instead, she felt emptiness, and her ears seemed to be ringing. Draken's betrayal had cut her as deeply as Bandon's death, perhaps more so.

A collar was placed around her throat. Bella didn't even flinch, but the clanging of the chains brought her out of her catatonic state. Suddenly, she realized she was on a platform and there was a mass of people before them. Guards kept them at bay at the bottom of the steps. All around them an army of Lycin and Yevik's soldier's stood at attention, a reminder that they were very much alone.

To her left, Azel and Aleron were bound as well, chains holding them in place, suppressing their abilities. Despite the circumstances and the gash on Aleron's forehead, they held their heads high. Then she saw it, the block at the end of the row. It was pale and covered in old chips and stains—an executioner's slab. The grief of losing a second love ached in her breast before joining with the cold chill of her own impending doom.

Aryia and the twins had been sent back to Sol under the guardianship of the trusted advisor–Hadish. Part of her worried if he could truly be trusted. Could anyone ever be believed again? A part of Bella died in that moment, a modicum of innocence that could never be regained.

The crowd fell into a hush as Lycin and Yevik stood before the crowd with Le'Roy between them. "People of Nova"—Yevik's voice carried across the still and attentive crowd—"this day at long last has come. The traitor and your Liege Aleron stands before you. Beside him is your greatest enemy, Azel Undel, who has been parading as your queen. They have forgotten what made Nova great, what made her powerful."

Bella felt a breeze against her cheek. She glanced up but saw nothing. Had that been her? No. She didn't feel her ability stirring. It was just her imagination. Closing her eyes against the scene, she realized what a desperate fool she was.

"Today you will be asked to follow the true way of the Corvinus Bloodline, a true son of both Sol and Nova, born here in this great city—Le'Roy Corvinus, son of Aleron and Lycin, both with the Corvinus Bloodline running through their veins." Yevik's speech was meant to move the crowd. He kept pointing at Lycin, beautiful and every bit a daughter of Nova. Her son carried the same features and had the bulk of a young man on the cusp of manhood. They were a perfect portrait of the Zendar of the past.

"Today will herald in a new time." Yevik's voice and gestures intensified. "We must wash away the old and bring in the new era."

"Bastard!" said a woman in the crowd, and then something smashed against the steps.

Craning her neck despite being hindered by the metal collar, Bella could see the rotted fruit. For the first time, Lycin appeared uneasy. She couldn't see Draken. Perhaps the coward could not face what his betrayal had done. Yevik did not hesitate, continuing on as though nothing had happened.

Shouting over the murmur in the crowd, he pointed an accusatory finger at Aleron. "His mother was a concubine like Lycin. Yet he is deemed fit to be your Liege?"

Bella glanced at Aleron. She'd known his mother was a concubine, but those had been different times. Her father had had three sons. The first, born from a queen, was killed in battle before Bella was born. The second had been killed by assassins the same night that her father fell and his betrothed was stolen. Aleron had been the only surviving son. Bella's mother had also been a concubine, though betrothed to be wed. It had taken nearly a year to track her down and rescue Bella. She shuddered at the memory.

Aleron had been but a boy when he'd taken control of Zendar. He grew up out for revenge, wanting to conquer all of Zendar so that it might bend to his rule and he could kill those who had taken his family from him. Until Azel. With Azel at his side, he had changed.

When the crowd began to yell, shouting for the release of Nova's true king and queen, Bella was not surprised. She watched Lycin and Yevik scramble for a moment, yelling to keep the crowd back. Chaos ensued as other people called for Aleron's and Azel's deaths. It was pure pandemonium, the cacophony of voices becoming an indistinguishable tangle. The stale air began to move as a short haired woman appeared—the one Bella had seen in the hallway on their ship.

When the crowd broke free of the guards, the woman's ability slammed against them. Such a display of power tempered the crowd enough that Yevik commanded in Aleron and Azel's direction, "Take off their heads!"

Bella's heart caught in her throat as she took a step back. Her bindings went taut. People tripped over themselves as they surged away from the group. Someone pointed in the air, and Bella saw the wall of sand.

Behind her, she heard the rattle of chains and a mighty roar from Aleron. Bella screamed as the wall crashed over the buildings and trees, spilling into the courtyard. She hunched down, bracing for the worst of it, certain it would slam against her any moment. Instead, she heard a strange noise, like a hum.

Thc sand had stopped beside them in a pile. Then, as quickly as it had come, it receded. Never before had she seen the power of the Bloodline Byden at work, and whomever yielded it now was immensely powerful. She looked up. Poised above the city in a small ship was a man. From the distance she couldn't make out his features.

"Kavil," Azel said under her breath.

Momby's Liege Kavil stood tall and stoic in the open side of a smaller airship. He held out his hands as the damage he had wrought was undone. Sand rolled out of the city and back into dunes of Zendar. Suddenly, someone shouted and charged them. Soldiers from Momby streamed through the crowd, but she could see they wouldn't make it in time to save them. Bella's hand clenched as the crowd began to climb onto their platforms. Suddenly, a man flew off the platform—Aleron, no longer chained, radiated merciless rage.

Ramas appeared in front of her, and suddenly she was free. There was screaming, people were attacking, and swords clashed—all was mayhem. Confused and unable to get her bearings, Bella shrugged off her chains and stumbled back.

She heard the wail of a woman in agony. It cut through the noise like a well-honed knife.

A disheveled Lycin was on her knees with Le'Roy on her lap. His eyes were open and vacant, his neck twisted at a strange angle. Bella felt sick—he was just a child! She'd loved him like family, cared for him when he'd been sick. She'd grown up knowing him, and now he was gone. Tears spilled down her cheeks as she stood, shocked to her core.

"My baby!" Lycin's sobs cut into Bella.

Aleron's voice sliced through it all. "Surrender, Lycin."

"Never!" Lycin screamed, and those who supported their cause began to attack.

"Then you will die!" Aleron's voice was like a thunderclap.

Lycin retreated into the interior of the palace with Le'Roy's body carried behind her by two men. Behind her, Azel no longer burdened by chains, went to stand beside Aleron. They glanced at each other, and Bella could feel the love between them.

"You knew..." Azel's words were somewhere between a question and a statement.

"I knew," Aleron confirmed.

"Our children?" Azel asked.

"Safe."

Azel seemed to consider his words and then slipped her hand into his. "Let's finish this."

When Azel and Aleron marched toward the palace together, Bella was entranced. Azel's dress danced in the breeze as she lifted one hand and men froze. Aleron took a fallen sword. Instinctively, Bella followed them. Most of Lycin's army was still within the palace, and Bella had to see it through—bear witness to the end.

She stayed close to them, following their trail of the dead and unconscious. When she reached the throne room, she saw Lycin standing in one of the windows. Bella's stomach knotted when she realized what was happening. Lycin's face was distraught as she took a step back, the transparent cape of her dress dancing behind her. Nothing but a sheer drop waited for her on the other side.

"Lycin, please." Azel's voice was surprisingly gentle. "Think of Verik."

A sob escaped Lycin's lips, and tear tracks marred her beautiful face. "You've ruined everything."

In an instant she vanished, falling to her death. Bella covered her mouth with her hands in devastation. Azel's head was bowed as Aleron put an arm around her. Azel fell into his embrace. A thought occurred to Bella as she stood on the threshold. *Verik.* He hadn't been in the courtyard. She ran to Azel and Aleron.

"Where is Verik?" she asked, breaking apart their tender moment.

"Draken took him," Aleron replied. "He promised to keep him safe when Kavil arrived." He said it casually, as though he hadn't just righted her world. As though the pain of Draken's betrayal hadn't just been eased a thousand fold by the sudden realization he'd never actually turned against Aleron.

"What do you mean?" She had to be certain.

"They are likely in Verik's room," Aleron said.

Azel crossed her arms. "There are still enemies here. We should try to find them. I do not know what Yevik's ability is. I could sense one within him, but I don't have Aryia's talent."

"Go with her. I'll see that this is done." Aleron didn't wait for Azel's reply, instead he kissed her soundly. Averting her gaze, Bella gave them a moment.

"You should have told me," Azel whispered.

"Did you sense my calm?" Aleron asked.

She hesitated. "I did."

"Then I did tell you." Aleron kissed her again before releasing her. "Be careful, Bella. Watch each other's backs."

Azel took her hand before Bella could dwell on his departure. The palace shook, and Bella knew a larger battle ensued beyond their walls. When they reached the second junction, a group of privateers attacked. Bella saw the horror and awesome power of the Vandi Bloodline as Azel cut through them. Azel made them turn their swords on each other, blades cutting flesh as it splattered the walls. Bella had to turn away, remembering there was a reason Azel and Aleron were perfect for each other. They had their own savagery that Bella didn't share.

Lost in thought, she stiffened when a hand covered her mouth. She sucked in a breath, ready to alert Azel, when a sharp tip pressed against her side. "Scream and you're dead." Yevik's hair was matted with blood, and his eyes were wild.

Bella was dragged backward away from Azel down the hallway. She tried to fight him but feared the blade against her back. A soft breeze followed them nonetheless. It only took her a moment to realize where they were going. They soon reached the hallway to Verik's room, where Draken was posted outside.

She whispered his name and earned a painful jab in her ribs. She gasped. She was sure he'd drawn blood. Draken's head came up at the sound, and she wanted nothing more than to run into the comfort of his arms. When he started forward, Yevik held her tight.

"If you come closer, I'll run her through." Yevik's words stopped Draken in his tracks. "Where is my son?"

"Inside," Drake replied, his voice with a sharpened edge to it. "Let her go."

"I knew you were sweet on her. Saw the way you pined over her in the throne room when she was being taken out." Yevik pointed the knife at Draken. "I should have guessed you'd betray Lycin."

Draken's hands tightened into fists. "Lycin betrayed our Liege. I requested clemency for her and her children. You have risked them needlessly." He took a step forward. "Do you think for an instant that the other Lieges would ignore the treaty?"

"It would have cost them their lives," Yevik snarled.

"No." Draken's voice was deathly quiet. "You do not know or understand the connection Queen Azel has fostered with the other Bloodline leaders. You would have paid for that mistake with Lycin's and my nephew's lives."

"Call to my son," Yevik commanded. "Or I gut her."

Though Bella could feel the point digging into her side, she felt calm. This was not how she was going to die. After everything, this was not where her life would end. There was so much she still wanted to do.

"Verik," Draken called out. "Come here, boy."

When Verik appeared, he was hesitant. Behind her, Yevik's tension felt like it lessened, as though he was relieved at the sight of his son. In contrast, Verik's face was drained of color and he appeared afraid. That was when Bella knew—he hadn't known about Yevik.

"Come to me," Yevik called. "We'll get your mother and go."

Verik held the door before shaking his head. "I don't want to." His face was twisted, and there were fat tears in his eyes. "You're hurting Bella. She's nice. Stop hurting her."

"I'll let her go if you come here," Yevik insisted.

He glanced up at Draken, who nodded solemnly. "All right," Verik whispered.

When Verik was close, Yevik shoved Bella forward. Her hands slapped against the ground and her knees cracked painfully a moment later. She looked back to see Yevik pull Verik against him. Draken started forward, but Yevik sprinted straight for the wall and disappeared through it. Bella's mouth hung open in astonishment.

"We have to stop him," Bella said, getting to her feet with Draken's help.

"I've never seen that," he replied tentatively touching the wall. "I don't know where they are going."

Bella remembered Yevik's words. "I do!"

Chapter 30:
"Zendar's Embrace"

Draken followed her down the hall. "Where?"

"He said they'd be going for Verik's mother." Bella glanced over, realizing what she was about to say. How could she tell Draken about his sister without hurting him? "She was in the throne room."

"Makes sense," Draken agreed.

When they reached a junction she paused and glanced up at him. It was strange to be so close to him after she was sure not too long ago that he'd betrayed them when he'd been working with Aleron all along. That he'd cast aside duty and honor for family. It didn't mean he loved her as she did him, but the pain was already subsiding. Bella knew she had to tell him about his sister before they arrived.

"She isn't there."

"Who?" Draken asked as they made their way down another hall.

"Lycin."

"Why?"

Bella took a steadying breath and gently touched his arm. "Le'Roy's dead, so she killed herself."

Shock registered on Draken's face and his jaw clenched. He ran a hand over his face. For a moment, it was like he'd shut down. Bella waited patiently and then, when he started forward again, followed. When they were nearly there, he stopped.

"You should stay here," Draken said, his expression grave.

"The last time I was left alone in a hallway, Yevik found me. I don't want to be left alone." As pathetic as it sounded, she was afraid, as much for herself as him.

He nodded. When they rounded the last corner before reaching the doorway to the throne room, Bella heard voices. Carefully, a step or two behind Draken, they went to the threshold. Inside, Yevik stood across the room with his hand on Verik.

"I promise I will care for him," Azel said, genuine concern in her voice.

"After what I let Titus do to you? You'll kill him to spite me," Yevik replied, his stance unyielding. "You may have everyone fooled, but I know what monsters Undels are."

"I learned a long time ago that we have to be the change we want to see in the world. Justifying evil deeds in the pursuit of a new world will change nothing," Azel replied. "Don't take my word for it. Ask the boy."

Yevik took a menacing step forward, pointing an accusatory finger at Azel. "Don't you try to use my son against me!"

Draken moved faster than Bella had expected. One breath he was beside her, and the next he was grabbing Verik and thrusting him back toward Bella. Yevik swirled and became translucent as Draken pulled his arm back to punch him. His well-aimed fist passed through him.

Bella shifted Verik behind her with shaking hands.

"Get your hands off him," Yevik yelled at her.

Draken tried to grab hold of Yevik, but the man let out a laugh and solidified his hand a second before it struck Draken's jaw. Though Bella was distressed, she focused on relocating Verik out of the room. Azel concentrated, eyes narrowed, but she seemed to have no effect on him. Then Bella realized he was like dust…or sand.

Falling to his knees, his face bloodied and panting, Draken appeared outmatched. Though Bella's ability was new and Yevik's ability terrified her, Bella had to try. The air began to move, and as she lifted her arms to her sides, a gale began to form. Her dress billowed and snapped in the wind. Her hair was wild around her face as the edge of Yevik began to pull away. Items crashed around the room as she saw him being pulled apart.

He reached his left hand into Draken's head. "Stop!" he screamed. "Or I end him!"

Torn, she hesitated and the windstorm teetered. "I will join my sister in death then," Draken replied, his lip bloodied and words slightly slurred. "Join her in Zendar's embrace."

Yevik looked shocked at hearing of her death. Before anyone could react, Azel appeared behind Yevik, her hands on his shoulders. Yevik grunted as she held his heart, blood covering her hand. It thumped, once, twice, and then stilled. Yevik went to his knees, caught between the transitions of his newfound ability, and then fell to piles of flesh. Azel stumbled, collapsing on the ground, awake but clearly spent.

Bella turned Verik away. “Don’t look.” His little hands covered his eyes as she shuffled him away. The wind quieted, and Draken fell back.

She was by his side in an instant, before she even realized she was going to move. Cradling his head in her hands, she cried out his name. He opened one eye, his face partially deformed and right eye mangled. A sob escaped her lips.

“You’re alive.”

He touched the side of her face. "I want one final smile."

“Don’t say that,” Bella managed, glancing up at Azel. “Please help him!”

“You promise me, you’ll live,” Draken said. The words seemed painful for him.

“Don’t speak.” She touched his lips as Azel crawled over. Tears blinded Bella.

“Promise…” His hand fell away.

She rocked over him, heart breaking into pieces. She’d lost him before she could tell him how she felt. Her world felt like it was ending. Her mind couldn’t accept what was happening. “I love you,” Bella whispered against his cheek, desperate to make him stay. “Please don’t leave me.”

Chapter 31:
"Blessings"

Bella wrung her hands outside the door where Draken lay. He'd been moved from his room to a guest room closer to the healers until he was completely out of danger. One final check, though, and he'd finally be free to return to his men and his command. It was her last chance, yet she hesitated. What if he didn't want her?

Her teeth scraped over her lip again and again as she vacillated. Perhaps it would be best to leave it well enough alone. No matter what she did, it wouldn't end well. Either he rejected her and it broke her heart or he accepted her and she'd have to tell Aleron. Both were not ideal prospects, but she wanted to try. Had to try.

Her fingers wrapped around the knob but she didn't turn it. She couldn't bring herself to. What would she even say? She could easily recall when he told her love and lust were hard to separate. And he'd kept secrets from her, even if Bella now understood why. Telling her could have ruined everything. It had wounded her, but what hurt more was the prospect of losing him. For a moment, after all, she'd thought she had.

"Bella?"

She jerked back at the sound of Azel's voice. Two of her handmaidens were on each side of her with trays in their hands. Bella took a few quick steps back, feeling like she'd been caught doing something bad. She suspected Azel had guessed at their relationship after seeing Bella's reaction when Draken had been injured.

Words were caught in her throat, but Azel's expression softened. "Go ahead. I'll be in to tend to him shortly."

The two women went past her and through the door she'd been so afraid to open. She craned her neck but could see only a dark room. When the door closed, she felt a sigh escape. Reluctantly, she turned her attention to Azel.

"Last treatment?" Bella asked, trying to divert the conversation.

"Last treatment," she confirmed, but her expression was coy.

Bella let the silence stretch out between them. "Good."

"Truly?" Azel asked, her eye critical. "You may have Aleron fooled, but not me."

Bella averted her eyes. "Don't be angry."

Azel lifted Bella's chin, her hand as warm as her smile. "Why in the world would I be angry?" Her entire presence radiated genuine support. "Does he make you happy?" Tears sprung to her eyes as Bella nodded. "Does he intend to marry you?" Bella shrugged, averting her eyes. "Do you want to marry him?"

This one was harder. She could see herself bound to him, but she didn't want him to agree out of duty. Only if he loved her. Her mind went to their moments together, the way he protected her and made her feel alive all at the same time. After a few moments she nodded ever so slightly.

"Then there is only one way to know for sure." Azel patted her shoulder. "Decide what you want to say and then do it."

Bella stared at the door blankly as Azel entered. Draken was propped up on the bed, his head bandaged. Seeing him hit Bella square in the chest. She'd checked on him regularly until he'd woken up, but after that she'd been too afraid to go back, acting like a frightened little girl.

Squaring her shoulders Bella lifted her head and steeled her spine. She marched into the room. Sunlight spilled across the bed and Draken. Azel was slowly unwrapping the bandage from his head. The door swung closed behind her, causing Azel to turn. Draken stared rigidly forward. She swallowed but moved to the end of the bed. Her hands worried together as she watched in anticipation.

"Will I keep the eye?" Draken asked. A yearning laced through Bella as she realized she missed his voice.

"Yes," Azel replied, "I was able to repair it, but it is unlikely it will work as well. You may be partially or fully blind."

Bella saw his hands tighten in the sheet, but he gave no response. Bella could barely breathe, her heart in her throat as she waited in anticipation. She fought to keep her tears at bay, her own discomfort forgotten in the face of his misfortune. When the last of the bandages fell away, Azel carefully removed the one over his eye.

The skin around it was still slightly bruised, but it was greatly faded. The eye itself appeared undamaged, but the way he swiveled his head around told her it wasn't working like it should. It was only then that he fixed his single working eye on her, apparently she'd been outside his view and he was only now aware she was there.

"The eye is a complex organ that may repair itself more over time." Azel bent to retrieve something from the tray. "I took the liberty of having an eyepatch made. During the day you should wear it, but take it off at night and when you are sleeping. If the eye improves, you can begin wearing it less; if it does not, I'd recommend you continuously wear it." Azel paused, glancing at Bella. "I'll leave you now."

Draken nodded as Azel waved the two servants out. Rooted to the spot, Bella was unsure how to comfort him. Azel paused to squeeze Bella's shoulder before leaving the room. Draken stared out the window, silent. His jaw was tight and his hands were still in fists.

She carefully made her way around the bed before sitting on it. Taking his right hand in her two, she gently lifted it toward her face. He turned slowly to her as she unfurled his hand and rested her cheek against it. Never before had she felt so close to him—they were both broken people now. Incomplete, but perhaps together they could be whole.

Bella sighed heavily. "I was afraid I'd never feel your hand again."

His fingers stretched out across her cheek, and she closed her eyes, letting the rough but familiar feel of them bring her comfort. "I'm sorry." Tears welled. "It was my fault."

"I'd do it again," Draken told her softly. Her eyes open at the tenderness in his voice. "No matter the cost."

A sob erupted as she threw her arms around his neck and drew him against her. Words were trapped as she held onto him. Slowly his arms wrapped around her, and he pressed his face against her shoulder. They stayed, entangled, neither willing to break their connection. They were still in that position when Aleron entered.

"I don't see why…" Aleron trailed off when he saw them.

Bella opened her mouth, her arms still around Draken's head and his hands on her back, but no words came out. It seemed they were not going to comply with her wishes today. Her first instinct was to move away from Draken, but she overcame it, if barely, and remained where she was.

"What is the meaning of this?" Aleron asked, his voice boiling with anger. His face twisted into the same mask of fury as he pinned his eyes on Draken. "What do you have to say for yourself?"

"Brother!" Bella began, putting a hand out in defense as Aleron came forward.

Before she could say more, Draken lifted her up and set her feet on the ground next to him. "Bella," his voice was calm. "Let me speak to my Liege alone."

She hesitated, wishing Azel were there to calm Aleron's anger.

"Go, Bella."

She reached down and took Draken's hand, shaking her head. "I won't leave you."

Aleron's glare focused on their joined hands. Suddenly, Azel was there. It took Bella a moment to realize she'd been in the doorway behind him. Unlike Bella, Azel didn't appear fazed.

Azel patted Aleron's arm. "Behave."

Aleron's rage lessened at her words. "I cannot promise anything."

Stepping directly in his path, Azel put her hands on her hips. "This isn't your choice. So you will listen." They glared at each other, and Bella held her breath. "Because I am asking you to do this for me."

That seemed to break Aleron's resolve. Azel rarely asked anything of anyone. It wasn't her way. It must have been the same for Aleron because he nodded, curtly. Seemingly satisfied, Azel turned back and reached a hand out.

"Come, Bella."

Bella's hand tightened on Draken's, and she felt him squeeze it back. Glancing down, she saw the pleading expression on his face. It was so slight that normally she wouldn't have noticed it. He had always seemed impossible to read, but now she saw it plain as day.

"All right." She squeezed his hand before following Azel from the room. She spared a glimpse at her brother, but his entire focus was on Draken. She turned and watched Draken from the hallway until the door clicked shut.

"This is a bad idea," Bella whispered, crossing her arms.

Azel had an amused smile on her face. "You've hurt his feelings."

"Draken seemed fine." Bella grumbled.

"Aleron's feelings, dear." Azel crossed her arms as well and jutted her hip out. "You are his darling sister, and you kept this big secret from him." Azel tilted her head. "How would you feel?"

Betrayed. Bella felt the word bounce from her mind down to her toes and back again. The memory of what Draken had done to her, the way he'd kept her in the dark. It had hurt, deeply, but she'd forgiven him because she could understand. It wasn't the same here, but she saw the parallels.

"Do you think he'll forgive me?" Bella's voice cracked, and she had to clear the emotion from her throat. "Forgive *us*?"

At the sound of a loud cracking, Bella immediately flung herself at the doorknob. In an instant she was in the room. Draken rubbed his jaw, and Bella yelled for them to stop. Her brother wasn't one to lash out, hadn't been for some time.

His voice was harsh. "I consent. If she'll have you." His footsteps were heavy as he approached Bella in the doorway. He paused and fixed his gaze on her. "You and I will have a long conversation about this."

Hand in hand, Azel and Aleron vanished. Bella realized her mouth was hanging open. She turned back to Draken, who studied her. Slowly she closed her mouth and tried to comprehend what was happening. When Draken beckoned to her, she went to him without question. He enveloped her in a hug. That feeling of home was a cloak of comfort. It made her feel hope.

"What did he mean?" Bella asked, leaning into him. "What did he consent to?"

"I am not a kind man, Bella." Draken detangled himself from her and held her at arm's length. "I will cause you pain, unintended, but it will happen." Bella was utterly confused, but she listened. "I've never trusted or needed another person. I've never felt lonely or like I was missing something. Even when Aleron changed, after Azel, I didn't want that for myself. I am what I am." Bella could remember him saying something similar when they were in Burtanian. "And then you almost died."

He leaned his forehead against hers.

"Draken, I don't understand. I know this already." She reached up and touched the side of his face. "Speak plainly."

"I want to protect you, now and forever." The words were hushed but firm. "I heard what you said when I was dying, and I asked the Liege for his blessing."

"Blessing?" Bella's heart swelled. He wanted to be with her. He'd asked Aleron for them to be together. "For us?"

He eased back, his face serious. "Yes." Tears in her eyes, she felt herself soar. "Will you consent to be my wife? To become my family." Bella's frozen, her fingers reaching to caress his face. Wife? She hadn't expected that so soon; hadn't expected it at all. "Bella?" His eyes were so hopeful.

"Drake…" How did she tell him? She likely couldn't have children, so there would be no family.

He immediately straightened. "I understand." He began to pull away from her, but she clamped down on his arms.

"You don't understand." She shook her head, her chest tight. "I can't give you a family. I cannot have children." She forced herself to meet his eyes as fat, hot tears rolled down her cheeks.

"I know you can't." Draken seemed baffled. "I was in the Liege's personal guard when he rescued you."

Bella hadn't remembered him. Most of that night was flashes of blood and terror. "You knew?"

"Yes." He searched her face. "Did you think I didn't?" She nodded vigorously. "Then you do want to be bound to me?"

"Yes." Tears streamed unabashedly down her cheeks as she buried her face in her hands. "I am truly blessed."

Bella felt his arms around her, and she moved to see his face. Draken kissed her softly, his beard brushing against her face. Extracting her arms, she threw them around his neck and pulled him closer. He chuckled as he lifted her up and spun her around. Bella let out an excited cry.

"I love you." Bella framed his face.

Draken kissed her soundly. "And I you, my Bella."

Notes from the Author

It was so amazing to be back on the sandy planet of Zendar. I hope you enjoyed the second book as much as the first. Bella was a new and different heroine then I normally write. She's a bit of a cry baby with a lot of spirit. Sometimes life is hard but if you keep trying you never know what you'll accomplish!

Six years in the making, Bella's story was always a possibility and thanks to the reviews and positive responses from fans, it's finally been told! The Zendar Collection has one more final book all outlined, ready for my attention. If you'd like to see more, make sure to leave a review mentioning the need to finish reading—only you can help make this happen.

In the meantime, happy reading,

K.T. Munson

Zendar: A Tale of Blood and Sand

Blood is how it all began, and only by blood can it end. Chaos has reigned in Zendar for years since the rise of the seven Bloodlines. The Liege Aleron Corvinus ruthlessly seeks revenge for the mistreatment of his ancestors. His ambitions will only be sated when he claims the world under his family's name; he will only stop when all of Zendar is his and the other six Bloodlines pay their weight in blood.

Azel Undel was born into this world of blood and sand. She is of a dying Bloodline, a feared one, but most coveted. Promised, in exchange for money, to a man she had never known; Azel travels across Zendar. Her ship is attacked and she alone survives, setting the wheels of fate in motion. She did not expect to become her enemy's captive or that he would demand her submission to him.

Loyalties are tested, secrets are uncovered, and Azel will have to make a choice: remain loyal to her family and everything she ever stood for or be loyal to her own heart.

Twitter: http://twitter.com/ ktmunson

Facebook: https://www.facebook.com/K.T.Munson

Subscribe to my blog:

http://creatingworldswithwords.wordpress.com

Made in the USA
Middletown, DE
02 July 2024